Waltham Forest Libraries

Please return this item by the last date stamped. The loan may be renewed unless required by another customer.

Jan 2020		

Need to renew your books?
http://www.walthamforest.gov.uk/libraries or
Dial 0333 370 4700 for Callpoint – our 24/7 automated telephone renewal line. You will need your library card number and your PIN. If you do not know your PIN, contact your local library.

Illustrations by Levente Szabo

PENNY CHRIMES

Tiger Heart

Orion

ORION CHILDREN'S BOOKS

First published in Great Britain in 2020
by Hodder and Stoughton

1 3 5 7 9 10 8 6 4 2

Text copyright © Penny Chrimes, 2020
Illustrations © Levente Szabo, 2020

The moral rights of the author and illustrator have been asserted.

A CIP catalogue record for this book
is available from the British Library.

ISBN 978 1 51010 704 5

Typeset by Hewer Text UK Ltd, Edinburgh
Printed and bound in Great Britain by Clays Ltd, Elcograf S.p.A.

The paper and board used in this book are made
from wood from responsible sources.

MIX
Paper from
responsible sources
FSC
www.fsc.org   FSC® C104740

To Scott and Holly,

Alexander and Sarah

For so much happiness.

And to Mum and Dad

For everything, always.

PART ONE

CHAPTER 1

Fly never meant to end up in the cage with a man-eating tiger. She just saw her chance to skedaddle, and she took it. And even when the cloud of soot cleared and she saw the golden eyes of a killer staring into hers, she still didn't straightway turn round and climb back up the chimney. 'Cos there was worse waiting for her back on the roof.

At least, she realised, looking at those teeth, the tiger would swallow her down in one bite and it would be all over quick. Instead of having bits knocked off her, day by day, 'til there was nowt left. She'd seen that done to others, and she wasn't going to let it happen to her.

'Well, this is a right pandalorum,' Fly said to the tiger.

When in doubt, say something. It was a bit of Fly wisdom that hadn't always worked out too well in the past.

But then she'd never been exactly in this particular boat of pickles before. And anything was worth a try. That was another bit of Fly wisdom. Not much more successful than the first, by the last count of her bruises under the soot.

The tiger looked like it agreed about the pandalorum. But it was saying nothing. Not yet, any road. It just stood still. Dead still. And stared at her with a steady golden gaze.

'You ain't stuffed, is you?' Fly asked, half-hoping, but half not. There'd be nothing to brag about over a stuffed tiger. She was already spinning this story in her head for later, how she'd tell the others, and they'd all stand round with their gobs hanging open like herrings. It'd be her best story ever, what would beat everyone else's stories into a flam-doodle. That was, if she lived long enough to tell the tale.

The tiger's long white whiskers twitched and it curled its black lips delicately, like it had tasted something that had disagreed with it.

'No offence, like,' Fly added quickly, seeing the look on the tiger's face. *Perhaps it didn't like the idea of being stuffed,* she thought, *and who could blame it?*

Any road, this tiger was most definitely alive. In the shadows of the stuffy cage, meanly lit through a patch of grimy greased-paper that passed for a window, the orange of the tiger's coat rippled and shifted and glowed like coals roasting chestnuts on a wet winter midnight. She wondered what it would be like to sink her fingers into its fur.

'You looks like you is made of bottled lightning,' Fly said.

The tiger stopped curling its lip and looked interested. *It likes a bit of flummery, then,* she thought.

'You looks like sparks would fly up me arms if I touched you.'

The tiger seemed to like that too. *Best tell it a story,* she thought. *Whiles we're chatting, it's not chomping on me, leastways.*

'There was this cove I saw, what had a show up the fairground, and he said he'd got bottled lightning in this fandangled machine he'd built. You had to hold on to the handles, both hands at the same time, and blimey! It fair frazzled off your fidgets!

'He was charging everyone a penny a shock – and they was queuing round the block!' Fly laughed and ruffled her short black hair until it stood stiff with soot like a devil's halo. 'Made your hair stand on end, like one of Black Bill's chimbley brushes.'

She stopped and looked at the tiger, which was still saying nothing. But it hadn't tried to eat her yet, either, and that was encouraging. It was then that Fly had one of her ideas. Fly's ideas didn't always work out too well, in the same way as her bits of wisdom often let her down. Like the rest of the gang of street urchins she reigned over, when she wasn't scraping soot out of chimneys Fly spent most of her time thinking up money-making wheezes. Being hungry and cold was a great encourager of wheezes.

'Here,' she said to the tiger, before giving the notion quite enough thought. Like, for example, how the tiger might take it. 'You and me, we could set up in business, down the fairground. "Step up, step up, penny a pat!" I bet they'd pay through the nose to have a go!'

Later on, Fly was to discover that the roar which exploded from the tiger's mouth at this point was *not* the most gut-shaking, rib-rattling roar in its repertoire. But it was loud enough for her to get the message that selling the tiger pat-by-pat in a fairground was not the best idea she'd ever had. In fact, at that moment, she thought that it might well be her last.

When the roar ended Fly was surprised to find that the walls were still standing and the ceiling above the cage had not fallen in. Equally, when it closed its mouth and opened its eyes – after what was by anyone's standards a pretty impressive roar – the tiger looked surprised to see that the

skinny, ragged, soot-stained girl who had fallen into its cage was still standing solidly on her two feet, her large black eyes staring steadily back into its own. She didn't even look scared.

'I'm sorry,' said Fly. 'That was a real nubble-headed notion. I begs your pardon.' One solid bit of wisdom Fly had learned in her mostly miserable and mostly hungry years on the earth was when to say sorry. At some ticklish moments out there on the streets it had saved her skin. But this was a tiger. Quite a touchy tiger. And she wasn't on the street. She was in its cage.

The space between Fly and the tiger shimmered with dust and possibilities. But Fly never considered simply turning round and climbing back up the chimney and facing another beating from Black Bill. She'd decided to run away, and once Fly had made a decision, she stuck with it. If she was unlucky enough to have run straight into the jaws of a tiger, then so be it. She was almost too big for the chimneys now, anyway. It was only a matter of time 'til her knees got stuck fast one day, and then no matter how much she wriggled she'd never get free. She knew Black Bill wouldn't be paying no one to knock down no walls to get her out. He'd just pack up his brushes and leave her there 'til she starved to death and dried up like a prune and fell down into someone's fireplace to be burned to a crisp. *That'd cause a proper palaver in the parlour, me dropping in for tea over the cucumber sandwiches!* she thought.

Besides, Fly didn't get on well with doubt and her stomach was rumbling. Black Bill had given her no breakfast when he woke her at blue o'clock in the morning, before shoving her up the first chimney as dawn broke over the rooftops, and now it was five chimneys on and she could hear the bells outside the window chiming for midday.

'You might as well get on with it,' she said to the tiger, impatiently. 'Look at it this way – neither of us will be starvacious no more. You'll be full up – or almost, 'cos I suppose I'm no more than a nibble for a king of beasts like you. And I won't be caring no more, will I?' Then she finished, more to herself than to the tiger, *At least I won't be going to bed with an empty belly, any road.*

It was then that the tiger moved.

Its stripes slipped through the soot-thick air towards her, sliding over shoulder bones that effortlessly shifted its weight from side to side. Its paws were like pudding plates, so massive they should shake the earth, but soundless as silk slippers.

The tiger's tongue curled out pink and its mouth yawned red and its teeth shone white, and Fly reckoned this was it, but it was a good way to go.

This'll give them something to talk about, down The Cut, come Saturday night, when I'm found in a heap of nobbut my bones, she thought. Fly liked the notion of being the talk of the streets, although she couldn't help feeling a twinge of disappointment that she wouldn't be around to fill in the details.

The tiger licked her left elbow where blood was oozing from the scrape of the bricks in the chimney. It felt as rough as a pumice stone on Fly's skin, but there was a warmth to it that she'd never felt in her life before. The lick took some soot off with it, leaving a black stain on the perfect pink of the tiger's tongue.

'Trying before tasting,' remarked Fly. 'That's smart. That's what I does, when I prigs a meat pie. I sticks my tongue in and licks out the gravy first, real slow. Lasts longer that way.'

The tiger looked up at her with unblinking eyes. It looked like it was puzzled about something. Then it bent its head and licked her knees. Its tongue was so big that one lick did for both knees. The grazes there were older and deeper, so many that Fly couldn't rightly remember which chimbley they'd come from. *The pain will come when the chewing starts*, she thought. *But maybe that'll be over nice and quick.*

Fly looked down at her legs. It might be the last time she would see them, and she was fond of them. They had got her out of a few scrapes, like when she needed to disappear fast after half-inching a pie or an apple off a stall.

The skin round the scrape, where the tiger had licked off the soot, shone clean and deep brown, dark against the ragged red of her scars. She only got to see her skin the right colour twice a year, when Black Bill's sour-faced cheese-box of a wife had to give her a wash, by law. That was no joke – she'd rather stay dirty than have her skin scrubbed raw by that mingy old trout. Sweeplings like her sometimes went for a dip to clean up in the Serpentine, but then someone told her that a boy got eaten by a corcodile, once, so she didn't go there no more. She'd never been much for the washing, anyway, even back at the workhouse.

The tiger looked up at her again, but this time it didn't look puzzled. It looked certain.

'Blue blood,' he said. They were the first words he'd said, but Fly wasn't surprised. She had somehow known all along that he could talk.

'Don't be daffy,' said Fly. 'Blood is red. It's just the soot, makes it look that way.'

'You have blue blood – *royal* blood – in your veins,' insisted the tiger, and he sank down and bent his knees and bowed his head to Fly.

'Your majesty,' he said. 'I hereby vow to restore you to your throne. However long it takes, and however wicked the enemies that stand in your way, you shall be queen.'

CHAPTER 2

'Fly! Get your scrawny little backside up here!'

Even if Fly hadn't already made up her mind to escape, Black Bill's bellow down the chimney was all the convincing she needed. She was certain sure of what was waiting for her on the roof if she went back up there.

'Where the devil is you, Blow-fly? You could have cleaned every chimbley in town by now, up and twice down again. Shift yourself, you little toe-rag, or I'll be scrubbing the floor with your face!'

Blow-fly was Fly's full name – or at least the only one she remembered – given to her by Black Bill out of the generosity of his heart. He'd always told her that she'd been born a maggot, and had grown up into a dirty fly. Her name was the only thing he'd given her since he'd bought her for a shilling from the workhouse and christened her into the ways of soot. She'd had nothing but a number before that, so having a name was a step up. The little gang of crossing-sweepers, mudlarks and tumblers that she'd gathered about her reckoned 'Fly' suited her anyway, because she was never in one place for long, and so it had stuck.

At the sound of Black Bill's voice, one of the tiger's round ears gave a twitch. Ripples of black and white and orange knitted into a deep frown across his forehead, and his pupils shrank to pinholes. Fly thought maybe he didn't like Black Bill's sort of talk any more than she did.

The bellow from the roof reminded her that she needed to scarper, before her master came down to find her. Usually he waited below for her, so when she'd clocked that he was staying safe up top today, that's when she'd seen her chance to escape. She could see now why he'd stuck with the roof.

'Look, mister, if you ain't peckish, I'll be off,' Fly said politely. If it wasn't for all this chin-wagging with the tiger, she would have been long gone by now. She started to sidle to the back of the cage, towards the patch of window that was next to the fireplace she'd landed in. The window – small though it was – looked like the most promising way out to the street. She'd not had much time to case the joint, but the cage had thick iron bars on three sides, bolted firmly to the wall. It faced on to a shadowy cavernous hall which echoed with strange shrieks and growls and cries that didn't sound like they rightly belonged here at all. Fly was certain sure she didn't want to meet whatever was lurking out there. A tiger was enough for one day. No, the window was the safest bet for someone accustomed to wriggling out of impossibly small spaces.

'But what about your kingdom, your majesty?' The tiger's voice rumbled deep as a dungeon in his barrel chest.

Fly stopped sidling and turned to look at him. From the droop of his whiskers, he looked like he was disappointed in her.

'Oh,' said Fly. 'I thought that was just a load of gammon. You must be mistook, mister. How can I be a queen? I'm just Fly.'

'It does seem unlikely,' agreed the tiger, 'given the amount of dirt. But blood does not lie. What is your parentage?'

Fly looked blank.

'My what-age?'

'Your parentage? Who are your ancestors? Who are your father and mother?'

'Blame me if I knows,' replied Fly. 'I was just found. Laid like an egg in a basket, outside the workhouse. Nobbut a year old, they said. But no one never said nowt about me being royal.'

There was another bellow from the roof, and Fly took a step closer to the window. It didn't really deserve to be called a window, but she'd got through smaller gaps when the crushers were after her, and there was no glass in this one to slice her skin to ribbons.

'Take me with you.'

There was something about the way the tiger said it that made Fly stop and look back. It was half-way between commanding and begging, and for the first time she twigged the woefuls in the tiger's eyes.

'How the devil am I going to take you with me? You'll never squidge through that windy.'

'But you could get through the bars of the cage.'

'And then what?'

'The keys.'

The tiger nodded to a row of hooks on the pillar opposite, from which were dangling a dozen sets of keys.

'Those are the ones. I've been watching.'

Fly considered. She reckoned she was skinny enough to get through the bars, any road. They'd been built to keep in a tiger, not a half-starved street urchin like her. But then what? There was something she'd heard on the streets about this tiger that was preying on her mind.

'Look, mister. Why should I take you with me? It just gives you more chances to eat me. Even if you ain't peckish now, you will be, come tea-time. It ain't in my own particular interests, see?'

'If I were going to eat you, I would have eaten you by now,' rumbled the tiger. 'Besides, I don't eat people.'

Fly looked the tiger straight in the eyes. It wasn't easy going eye-to-eye with a tiger, but she wasn't a girl to scare easy.

'Now, see, I knows that ain't true. 'Cos I heard about you. You is the one what broke out, down by the docks, and ran down the street and grabbed that little lad's noggin in your grinders.'

The tiger dropped his golden gaze.

'That was just a misunderstanding,' he muttered. 'I was never planning to eat him.'

'Well, you can see how it might have looked that way to him, what with his noggin stuck down your gob, staring at your tonsils.'

The tiger looked up, defensive. 'I had been locked up in a crate for many months, after wicked men from my country caught me and took me to a ship's captain. He shut me in a cage and brought me here over the sea. When the ship docked, they left the crate open for a moment, and I took my chance at freedom. But then there were so many people, and I didn't know which way to run.

'The boy got in my way. So I picked him up in my mouth, like a cub. I could have swallowed him down in one bite, but I didn't hurt a single hair on his head!

'But then a cruel man came and hit me with an iron bar, over and over, and all was darkness. When I woke, I was a prisoner once more.'

The tiger's great head was bowed so low that Fly could hardly hear him. 'I have been shut up here ever since. Have I not been punished enough? What do they want with me? This place is so cold and grey. My land is full of bright colours and sweet smells that hang in the air so you can almost taste them . . .' His voice was so full of longing, Fly could almost taste them too. He sighed. 'I long for my country, to return to my homeland, but I think they will keep me a prisoner in this dark place until I die.'

Fly knew all about being trapped in the dark. She remembered when her waistband had got caught on a broken brick half-way down a chimney and the panic had taken hold and her breath had been like a wild animal trying to bust out of her chest. It had taken all the courage she'd had to stop herself screaming and to work out that the only way out was to buff it and wriggle out of her rags. She'd ended up popping out of the fireplace in nothing but her Adam and Eve's.

Fly knew then that there was no way she could leave the tiger to die of despair, here in the dark. So she stopped thinking about that window and stepped over to the front of the cage. She almost tripped over the remains of a carcass attached to a pair of hairy grey legs in the corner. The legs looked familiar.

'Last time I saw them legs they was fastened to Pardiggle's donkey, what pulls the milk cart,' she remarked to the tiger. 'It didn't look too good then, but it looks a lot worse now. So that's why you ain't hungry!'

Fly slipped between the bars like a hot knife through butter. 'Good job I ain't nobbut a bag of bones,' she said.

She could, of course, have just kept going and left the tiger behind. But when she turned back and looked at him, her dark eyes were sparkling with excitement. There was nothing Fly liked better than an impossibility.

'What next, mister? Once I gets my dib-dabs on the keys?'

'The guard is always drunk by now,' said the tiger, with that disapproving curl of his lip that Fly was beginning to recognise. 'He only wakes up when his master comes to inspect us. Or when customers come to buy.'

'Gin for breakfast, dinner and tea, I bet.' Fly nodded. She knew about the ways of gin. You couldn't grow up as a gutterling and not know the ways of gin.

'We can just walk past him,' said the tiger.

It wasn't as elaborate a plan as Fly would have liked. She liked a bit of trickery and daring and a flying-by-the-seat-of-her-pants sort of plan, but she had to admit this had a simplicity about it that might just work.

The hooks for the keys were too high for her to reach, so she dragged a bale of bedding straw over and hopped on top.

'It is the key on the end,' said the tiger. There was something new in his voice, which sounded like hope.

Fly came back with a heavy iron key. It slid smoothly into the lock and turned without a sound. The tiger stepped out of the cage, and Fly almost went topsy-turvy into a pillar as he gave her a nudge with his great head, like an over-grown kitten.

'Thank you, your majesty,' he said.

'Look, we ain't out of this pickle yet,' replied Fly quickly. 'And I reckons you should hold off on all that majesty stuff until I gets my kingdom.' She was thinking what the others would say if they heard talk of her royal blood. 'That sort of chat will go down on the street like a bucket of rotten tripe.'

Anyway, she didn't want to hurt the tiger's feelings, but she didn't believe for a moment in any future kingdom. A good day for Fly was getting through twenty-four hours with a bite to eat, and somewhere to sleep at the end of it, away from Black Bill's beatings. Today it would be a good day if she made it to sunset without Black Bill catching her and laying her out flat as a flounder. Leave alone how she was going to find somewhere to kip with a full-grown tiger in tow.

She locked the cage behind them and hung up the key. 'That'll flummox them for a bit,' she snorted. 'They'll think as you've gone up the chimbley in a puff of smoke.'

The tiger's cage opened on to a kind of pillared arcade that ran all the way around the sides of the building. More bars stretched away to each side, and Fly could hear rustling and low moans and growls coming from the cages. She peered into the shadows. The dim light shone back from so many sets of eyes she couldn't count them. 'Blimey!' she muttered. 'There's so much sadness in them eyes, you could bottle it and never run dry.'

Fly stepped out between the pillars and looked up. The building was as high as a church, not that she'd had much call to be inside many churches, but she'd stared up at their spires from the gutter. A narrow landing with railings ran round the whole building, and above it, hanging from the grimy glass ceiling, dangled a thick fishing-net.

Birds as bright as bits of broken rainbow were beating their brilliant wings against the glass, cut off from escaping by the net below. They were desperate to get to the open sky above.

'Cor, them's no spadgers!' She whistled between her teeth.

These birds were nothing like the tattered brown sparrows with whom Fly had many a time shared a gutter and a crust on the streets of London. These birds were calling to each other with harsh wild cries and Fly reckoned she knew what they were saying to each other. 'Keep trying!' 'Don't give up!' 'The sky is just up there!' She could feel their hearts busting in their chests. *That's how I felt, when I got trapped back there in that chimney.* Some of the birds had exhausted themselves and had fallen, senseless, to the netting below.

Fly's eyes blurred. As she blinked them clear, a feather the colour of flame fluttered past and drifted to rest on her bare feet. When she looked down she realised that the floor was thick with feathers, which lit up the grey building with colour. She hadn't felt their softness beneath the street-hardened soles of her bare feet.

The cries of the animals were all different, but she guessed they were saying the same thing as the birds: 'Take us with you!' and they were pressing in on her until she had to lift her hands to cover her ears. She bent down and tucked the scarlet feather in her pocket, like a silent vow.

This was a new feeling for Fly. She'd never felt any obligation to look out for anyone but herself before. In her world, anyone would cheat anyone out of anything if it meant getting to the end of the day with a full belly. Money was all, and a few pennies made you a king on these streets. Those were the rules, and everyone knew the rules.

She turned back to look at the tiger, who was watching her from the shadows. 'What is this place?' she whispered.

'They call it a menagerie. It is full of creatures from my country, captured by the same wicked men who caught me.' The tiger shook his great head and flashes of anger leaped from him like the white-hot sparks from a blacksmith's anvil.

'Her majesty will come back for you all,' he growled softly to the animals, under his breath. 'She will not forget you.'

He's precious fond of making promises for me that I'll never be able to keep, thought Fly. But it was a relief to have the decision about the other poor creatures taken away from her, because Fly had no idea where she would put them all. For that matter, she had no idea where she was going to put a tiger. Or herself, now she'd escaped from Black Bill.

Or had she?

Fly and the tiger were about to step past the snoring sapskull of a guard, when a great banging came at the human-sized door that had been cut into the elephant-sized ones that stretched from floor to ceiling.

The old man spluttered back to consciousness and lurched to his feet before what was left of his gin-sodden brain caught up and warned him that he hadn't done up his belt. As he started for the door, sending empty gin bottles clattering around him, his trousers tumbled down and trapped him by the ankles, and he went sprawling to the ground. He lay there flapping like a bluebottle stuck on a jam sandwich.

'I'm a-coming, I'm a-coming,' the guard spluttered as he struggled to work out why he was trussed up like a turkey on the floor.

'He's too tossicated to fasten up his kecks!' Fly snorted with laughter. But then the banging got even louder and Fly knew that Black Bill had started ramming his block of a head against the wood in frustration. She'd heard it often enough before, wrapped in her blanket under the kitchen table, when he'd come home half-seas over and his wife had locked the door against him. Those were the nights when he took it out on Fly with an extra beating. It would only be a matter of time before his massive bull shoulders followed his head though the wood and Fly would be getting the larruping of her life.

'Croopus! He's in a rare old humdudgeon,' she said to the tiger. 'Time for us to scarper.'

Another bit of Fly's street-wisdom was never to find herself anywhere without knowing the whereabouts of at least two exits, should the need arise, as it often did. She already knew there was a metal staircase that led up to the gallery at the other end of the building. And she knew that it would lead to a fire escape, sure as eggs is eggs.

She led the way. Some instinct still held her back from touching the tiger, some sense told her that was a liberty too far, even for someone who had recently been told that she had royal blood. But the tiger followed her without hesitation, and she could feel the hot breath from his great mouth on the back of her bare legs as she bounded up the wrought-iron steps.

At the moment they burst out on to the fire escape and into the fresh air – or as fresh as London's spewing chimneys and stinking sewers had to offer anyway – Black Bill burst into the menagerie below. He was looking more wild and savage than any of its caged inhabitants. 'Where's that good-for-nothing brat?'

But the good-for-nothing brat was already dancing her way along the rooftops in the late spring sunshine high above his head, as swift-footed and certain as the great beast that padded after her, rejoicing in the movement of every unconfined muscle.

Fly thought she was free.

She didn't see, because she'd never seen it, the dark figure that slipped silently though the streets below, shadowing her every move. It had followed her every moment of her life since she was brought to London many years before, years before her remembering. It knew where she was, as certain as seeing, but without needing to see. It was too small to be human, but it possessed an intelligence and a purpose that had been conjured by a human mind of immense evil.

It was a golem. Whose task it was to haunt Fly's every step and never let her go. And to keep her from her birthright.

CHAPTER 3

''Tis a penny for you, and a farthing for the dog . . .'

There are those people who might have thought twice about boarding an omnibus with a fully grown tiger, in broad daylight or otherwise. But those people were not Fly. She couldn't remember a time when she couldn't do the seeing trick, or more accurately, the not-seeing trick. People, quite simply, saw what Fly wanted them to see, and never saw the rest.

'You is joking, mister! A farthing for me dog?'

'Taking up a seat, ain't it? Dog that size – ought to be a law against it!'

Fly paid the conductor from her precious little store of coins, and she and the tiger went and sat down at the front of the omnibus, behind the horses.

'Putting the stares on', as Fly called it, had many a time been the difference between eating and going to bed hungry, as she'd thieved her way around the crowded stalls of the city. It was her thing, and the feral little animal she had grown into never gave a second thought to the rights and wrongs of how she used – or misused – her power. Or even what that power was really for.

So now the conductor – and the rest of the passengers – saw nothing but a grubby little sweepling and a large dog. And the mutters of disapproval were more about Fly and her soot-stinking rags than about her pet. 'Shouldn't be allowed,' observed one plump woman with a face like a pig in a pink bonnet. She felt it wasn't a comfortable thing, to be reminded of how one's chimneys were kept clean. And one didn't pay good money to be made to feel uncomfortable on the number 10 omnibus.

The tiger shifted next to Fly and she felt his warm weight pressing against her thin legs, like a promise. She wasn't accustomed to being touched without it hurting.

'You lied,' the tiger observed. There was that twitch of disapproval on his lips again.

'Cricum jiminy!' Fly protested. 'What do you want me to do – prance on board and tell them to shuffle up and make room for me tiger? You'd be back in pokey in no time!'

The tiger looked away. He knew without telling that Fly had the power to control what people saw, and that she was using that power to protect him. But as he walked beside her, he saw the shadow that was following her, which she could not see. And he knew there would come a time when he would need to protect her against its unimaginable evil.

He stored the knowledge away, and fixed his gaze on the horses' fat rumps.

In Fly's opinion, the tiger was taking a bit too much interest in the horses. It wasn't easy for her to put the stares on animals. They weren't so easily bamboozled as humans. And these horses were getting decidedly twitchy as they got a whiff of tiger, full on their chests.

'Whoa, lads!' Try as he might, the driver was having trouble holding their heads. Londoners born and bred, these horses had never met a tiger, but they knew that whatever was sitting behind them was not their normal type of customer. And some ancient instinct was telling them that, unlike their normal customers, this one was thinking about eating them.

The omnibus picked up speed until it was careering down the street like the hounds of hell were after it.

'Here, Harry!' shouted the conductor. 'What's the hurry?'

There was a growing restlessness on board. Even the best-upholstered bottoms were getting bruised on the wooden seats as the omnibus rattled over cobbles and took the corners on two wheels, and Fly sensed that the general discontent was starting to focus on her and her large tawny companion.

'It ain't right!'

'What's a filthy sweep doing on an omnibus, in broad daylight? Ain't there no chimneys need cleaning?'

'Stop it,' hissed Fly to the tiger.

'What?' The tiger tore his eyes off the horses for a moment to look at her.

'You know what!' whispered Fly. 'You is frighting them horses into convulsions!'

If tigers could shrug, this one did now. And he had a point, thought Fly. He was a tiger, on an omnibus. How could he help it if he was scaring the horses?

It was becoming increasingly difficult for Fly to concentrate on keeping up the stares. If she let it slip there'd be a right to-do. The tiger would end up back behind bars, and as for her – if you could be hung for nicking a sheep, certain sure she'd be strung up for stealing a tiger. And she didn't want to end up swinging from Newgate gallows.

'Wotcher! Fly!' A shout came from outside the window.

'It's the tumblers!' cried Fly in relief. 'Come on!'

She led the tiger to the back seats, and the sweating horses slowed to a bewildered amble.

Keeping pace with the omnibus, three ragged lads were turning cartwheels and flipping handsprings along the pavement, waving or whistling according to which way up they were. Laughter and pennies were being showered on them by the passengers, and they sprang after the coins and grubbed them out of the gutter.

'Look at you, the lardy-dardy lady on the omnibus!' the smallest of the boys called as Fly got down. 'And what's that you've got . . .' His voice faded into confusion as the tiger leaped down after her.

Fly hadn't been quite quick enough to put the stares on the tumblers and the three of them gaped at the tiger for a moment, before she did her trick with the not-seeing. She didn't want too many questions here in the street. Time enough to tell them later.

'Black Bill's after me!' she said quickly. 'I has done a bunk! We needs somewhere to hide.'

Forgetting what they thought they'd seen, the tumblers stood before her in a row, skinny as skittles. Between them, they might have had enough rags to make a whole garment, but, shared among three, there was more hole than cloth.

They jangled the coins in what was left of their pockets and considered Fly's predicament.

'That's all rug, disappearing you, Fly, but how is we going to hide that mutt?' asked the tallest of the three. Stick's trousers had long ago given up the fight to make the acquaintance of his jacket, no matter how often he tried to hitch them up. His face was as long and thin as his body, but it was lit, beneath jet-dark hair and brows black as beetles, with a grin and grey eyes that twinkled bright as brimstone.

'Seen jumbos smaller than that, up the circus!' the middle skittle joined in. They called him Spud on account of the pockmarks, left by a near-death brush with smallpox, which made him look like a spotty potato. He was also the roundest of the three, always being the quickest when it came to the prigging of grub. A choir-boy smile distracted his victims from his thieving and pocket-picking. He was wearing with pride a grey wool cap, lifted from the unconscious head of a drunk the night before; it was the only hole-free item between the three of them. It was the envy of the other tumblers and Spud knew it could not be his for long. The new cap was wedged on top of what might have been fair hair, if soap and water had ever seen it.

'What's that thing eat?' the smallest of the skittles demanded. Food was never far from Sparrow's mind. No matter how much he managed to beg, borrow or steal, he was always hungry, but he never seemed to grow any bigger. Being small, Sparrow had barely been able to walk before he was put to work by a house-breaker, on the grounds that he could be shoved through any window and then sneak round to open the door. But the work hadn't suited Sparrow, who didn't see why he should risk his neck stealing stuff for other people. First chance he had, he'd chosen the wild and dangerous freedom of the streets and turned his skills to tumbling instead.

Being small, Sparrow should have had a better chance of his rags meeting round his middle, given that they had less to cover. But he was always last in line when it came to the hand-me-downs, so there wasn't much left by the time the togs got to him. What had once been a toff's tweed coat was frayed into cobwebs and was very much lacking in sleeves; his elbows stuck out like the bones of a bird, which is how he got his name.

Fly dismissed their questions impatiently. 'Never mind all that now – where can we go? I needs to get off the street afore Bill catches up with me.'

'There's that crib what we used to kip in down by the river,' said Stick doubtfully. 'Unless it's floated away.'

'It were full of pigeons and rats!' objected Sparrow. 'Bold as brass and big as cats, them rats! They was almost as big as me!'

'They ate the only pair of boots I ever had, right off me feet,' mourned Spud. 'Went to sleep with them on, woke up in the morning and the boots was gone. Nothing left but the buttons. Only woke up when they started tickling me toes with their whiskers.'

Fly shivered. There wasn't much that scared her, but she had no time for rats. And pigeons were just rats with wings on. Then she looked at the tiger and saw the solution.

'Don't reckon as the rats will be a problem for long, with him around,' she said. 'Nor the pigeons. Show us the way.'

The tumblers' old crib, Fly discovered when they got there, was an abandoned warehouse, overhanging the dark and dangerous waters of the Thames. The buildings round it had fallen down long before. It stood on a low-lying mudflat, leaning over the water as if it had abandoned all hope and was planning to plunge in and end it all at the bottom of the river.

'Croopus, that ain't too shummocky, lads!' remarked Fly. 'One puff of wind and we'll end up in the drink!'

'Private, though, like,' observed Stick. 'No one's going to be bothering you for the rent!'

'They'd have to be barmy,' agreed Fly. 'And it's better here than being walloped into next Wednesday by Black Bill.'

Nobody fancied going round to the front steps, which had lost touch with the tow-path and were hanging right out over the river. Sparrow gave a shout and they trooped round the other side to find him, watching out for broken glass in the river mud that lay thick around the walls. A twisted iron staircase dangled from the first floor like a caterpillar, leading up to an open doorway.

'Reckon we can skip up that like a flock of little lambs,' said Sparrow. 'Not so sure about that dog.'

They all looked at the tiger.

The beast had padded quietly behind them along the bustling pavements and down the maze of alleyways that narrowed as they got closer to the river. No matter how the crush of people pressed in around them, the tiger had slipped through the crowds without touching anyone, sinuous as a stream of pure gold winding through the grey streets. It was only Fly who noticed the curl of his lip when she used her cloud of unseeing to nick food from the stalls as she went.

At no point had the tiger done anything to upset anyone's illusion that he was just a big dog. But now he took a long look at the rickety staircase and gave himself a great shake, before leaping effortlessly six feet up to the doorway.

'Cor blimey!' Spud whistled in awe. 'A flying dog!'

Fly swung herself lightly up the staircase after the tiger, and snorted as she looked back at the bewildered tumblers below.

'Look at you, gaping like a bunch of jobberknolls! Get up here. I'm nibblish hungry!'

It seemed like she wasn't the only one that was hungry. By the time the boys joined them, the tiger was gambolling about, clearing the place of rats, skewering three at a time with a single swipe of an immense paw. He looked happy to be eating stuff that had a pulse for a change. The pigeons had already taken flight to the rafters and were cooing anxiously to each other, plotting a swift escape.

Fly was too busy unpacking the stolen picnic from her pockets to bother keeping up the stares, and she left the tumblers to work out for themselves how they had ended up in the same room as a tiger.

'Here, Fly, that ain't no mutt . . .' Sparrow was clearly torn between scoffing the picnic and making a run for it.

'You must be loose in the basket, Fly, bringing us here with that,' protested Spud. He eyed the growing pile of rat's tails on the floor. It seemed the tiger wasn't so keen on tails.

Mebbe they gets stuck between his teeth, thought Fly.

'I'm off before he starts on me,' Sparrow said.

The pair of them looked as nervous as the pigeons.

'That's the cove as tried to eat that little lad,' observed Stick, calmly. He'd heard the same street-story as Fly. But he made no move for the door, and Fly grinned. She knew Stick would be as game for a lark as she was, and wherever Stick went, the other tumblers would follow.

'He was locked up in this place what was like pokey but for animals – there was all these creatures, like what you've never seen before, stripy horses like humbugs, and things with necks as long as ladders, and monsters with great humps on their backs, and dragons that breathed fire and such like . . .'

The tiger stopped bounding after the rats and gave Fly a look.

'Mebbe not dragons,' she said quickly. 'But any road, he was breaking his heart, all locked up in the dark. I couldn't have left him there, could I?'

The tumblers shook their heads. They knew about being locked up. They all knew gutterlings like them that had been caught by the crushers and put in chokey, or worse, transported to 'Stralia – where everyone knew the natives walked upside down – and were never heard of no more.

They all lived with the daily fear of being caught picking pockets. It was only a fast pair of heels and Spud's choir-boy smile that had kept them out of the clutches of the police so far.

'Besides, he's quite safe,' Fly went on. 'He's promised he won't eat us.'

Emboldened, Spud and Sparrow took a step closer to the tiger. Only Stick remained where he was, leaning, one foot bent behind him, against the slanting wall. He chewed calmly on the stem of an unlit pipe he'd produced from his pocket, his grey eyes intent on the tiger. Fly could see him thinking it all through. He was the thinker, was Stick. It was always him and her that came up with the best wheezes.

'What are you going to do with it, Fly?' asked Spud. His first thought, as Fly's had been, was how to turn the tiger into a nice little earner.

Sparrow's face lit up. 'I knows!' he cried. 'We could take it up to Hampstead Heath and charge the toffs' kids tuppence a ride. That'd knock them donkeys into a cocked hat.'

Before Fly could tell him to mash it, Sparrow found himself flat on his back on the dusty warehouse floor, with the tiger's pudding-plate of a paw pressed down on his chest and a set of claws flexed a whisker from his windpipe.

'I forgot to tell you, he's a bit touchy, lads,' Fly said quickly, and then to the tiger, 'He don't mean no harm, mister, he's just a totty-headed little tyke, what can't tell a king of beasts from a pedlar's moke.'

Sparrow glared at Fly, but the tiger slowly sheathed his claws and let the boy scramble to his feet. Sparrow and Spud shuffled back towards the door in case the tiger took offence again.

There was a silence, broken only by the rising tide lapping against the walls of the warehouse and the scurrying of the remaining rats under the floor.

'So what *is* the plan then, Fly?' Stick hadn't shifted from his spot, propping up the wall.

Fly had known all along, really, ever since she'd taken the tiger in tow and ever since she'd picked up that scarlet feather. But she'd not said it out loud, even to herself.

'We takes him back home, of course.'

Fly looked at the tiger, and the tiger looked at Fly.

'Wherever home is.'

CHAPTER 4

That night, under a moonlit sky, the tiger taught Fly to swim.

The tumblers had gone. Time was money and as evening drew on, there were toffs to tumble for outside the theatre. Fly had many times watched them putting on their nightly show for the swells, done up all dandy in their top hats and tails. The toffs were always more free with their tips if the tumblers could make them laugh when they had a pretty lady on their arm.

'See you tomorrow, Fly!' called Sparrow and Spud as they leaped down the staircase and paddled in their bare feet through the shallows that now cut off Fly's new crib from the street. They looked like they couldn't get away fast enough. But Stick lingered longer. He hadn't taken his eyes off the tiger.

'What you going to feed him on, Fly? He can't eat nowt but rats.'

Fly knew Stick was just thinking out loud; he'd already have a plan.

'I'll drop by the meat stalls down Smithfield, after the show,' he said, casually. 'See as if I can give something a bit of help falling off the back of a cart. Bit of bow-wow mutton or suchlike.'

'Or them bags of mystery they calls sausages!' Fly grinned. 'Don't reckon as he'll be too particular, as long as he gets his grinders into some solid prog.'

And then Stick was gone, and Fly was left alone with the tiger. As the dusk drew on, she could feel the rickety wooden building shifting on the rising tide as if it was a ship on its moorings, making the whole place creak like a sinner drawing his last breath. When she peered through the floorboards, there was nothing but water below.

'Here, watch it!' The tiger had bounded after another rat and as he pounced with his full weight, the warehouse rocked towards the river. 'Best stay up this end, mister. We don't want to end up in the wet – be better off sailing down the river in a sieve!'

Fly huddled up with her back to the wall. Some of the shine was going off this adventure. The rest of the gang would be curling up together for the evening in doorways and church porches, with whatever hot vittles they'd prigged, trading wild tales about the narrow escapes of their day. They were the best times, when she slipped out to join them on the nights Black Bill was too tossicated to remember to lock the door.

'Cor, what a slumdinger of a story I'd have to tell them tonight,' she said to herself, wistfully. ''Stead of which I is perched up here in a bird's nest that's rocking about like it won't last 'til dawn.' And then she thought, *With a tiger what might any minute take it into his head to eat me,* but she didn't say that bit out loud. *Don't want to go putting ideas in his bonce. Like Stick says, them rats ain't going to fill his belly for long.*

But then she shook herself. Anything was better than going to bed with a fresh black eye and a stale crust of bread and nothing to look forward to but another day shimmying up and down chimbleys with Black Bill's brush up her backside.

'I'll never have to nick nothing for that greedy skinflint no more,' she promised herself. Black Bill was always mithering on at her to pocket any trinkets and gee-gaws left lying around in the toffs' bedrooms, after she was done cleaning their chimbleys. In Fly's head, it was one thing to steal food to survive. But she'd never felt easy about the whole havey-cavey business of stealing their precious things, just to fill his pockets.

She breathed in deep. She was free. And she was going to stay free, whatever it took.

Fly looked over at the tiger. He was standing, framed by moonlight, at the threshold of the open doorway. As she watched, he lifted his nostrils to scent the damp night air, and she knew that, like her, he was smelling freedom. He shook himself and a cloud of bright hairs rose in a moonlit halo around his great head, before being snatched up by a sea-bound breeze. He turned to watch them blow away past the forest of ships' masts and rigging, towards the distant east.

'Blowing east. Blowing home,' the tiger said softly, as Fly joined him at the doorway. 'This is the time when the animals gather at the waterholes . . . the smell of darkness will be rising from the earth . . . the promise of the hunt will be in the air.' His head drooped, defeated. 'But I cannot smell it here. This is the time when I miss my homeland the most.'

Fly reached out but she still didn't touch him. She stood as close as she dared, for comfort. His or hers, she didn't know.

A silence stood between them.

Then the tiger's head turned and his nostrils twitched again, but this time there was a wrinkle of disapproval. 'But I *can* smell you . . .' And with a playful nudge of his head, the tiger knocked Fly down into the river.

'I can't—'

'Swim' is what she was going to say, but the word was lost under the green depths of the Thames. She'd never got on with water, and imaginings of corcodiles and sea monsters flitted through her head as she watched the bubbles bearing her last breaths up to the surface. Her chest was bursting and still she was sinking . . . down, down. She could feel weeds clutching at her bare feet like slimy fingers . . . but then . . . *I'm blowed if I is going to die like a gutter-perch down here!* Fly kicked desperately for the silver circle of moon floating above her head. At that moment she felt herself being lifted from beneath, and her head burst out of the water just as the tiger's head came up beside her.

She barely had time to draw breath before a great paw smacked down next to her and sprayed her with water, and then the beast reared up and seized her and rolled her back under. Over and over, every time she surfaced, spluttering and swearing every oath in her wide repertoire, the tiger was on her again, rolling her around like a pair of drawers in a dolly-tub.

For a long and terrible moment Fly believed the tiger was actually trying to kill her. She remembered that boy he'd got in his grinders, down by the docks. *I must've been a complete nick-ninny to be codded by a tiger,* she thought, in panic.

But then she managed to get her head above water again, and she saw that he was grinning. And at last it dawned on her that this was a game.

'You is just playing, ain't you?' she spluttered, and now she'd worked out that her legs would always kick her back to the air, and that the tiger wasn't trying to drown her, Fly splattered a wave of water back into the tiger's face.

With a laugh that came out as a roar, he was on her again, and rolled her back under, until she struggled back up and dived on to his head, dunking it below the waves. Her legs caught against his flank as he swam underneath her, and she dared to spread her feet to stand on his broad back until he shook her off and sent her plunging back down again. She was laughing too, now.

They might have stayed there playing all night, as the years of ingrained soot and filth lifted from Fly's skin and floated away in a dark cloud down the river. But at

last the tide began to fall and she was shivering so much that the tiger nudged her back to the shore. He stopped at the water's edge and stared hard along the bank, as if he was searching for something in the shadows, while Fly waded through the mud and climbed back up the metal staircase.

'Croopus! I'm perishing!' Fly was shaking, her thin rags clinging to her bony frame. She stripped them off and hung them over the railings in the breeze, but then she remembered something: 'The feather!'

It was still there in her pocket, a bedraggled smudge of scarlet. She took it out, blowing on it softly, and wrapped it tight in her palm to dry it out. But she was getting colder and colder without her rags. For a moment she thought longingly of her threadbare blanket under the kitchen table at Black Bill's.

The tiger leaped up behind her, sending a spray of moonlit droplets cascading back to the river behind him. And then, without a word, he started on the task of licking Fly dry like a cub, his rough tongue making her freezing skin glow warm as bread on a toasting fork. It was like all the mothering and fathering Fly didn't even know she'd missed, and for some reason her cheeks were suddenly wet again.

'Your skin is brown, not like the pale people who live on these cold streets,' the tiger said, when he was satisfied she was dry. 'Do you know nothing of where you come from?'

'I told you!' Fly scrubbed the back of her hand over her eyes, angry without rightly knowing why. 'I was just found, outside the bone-shop – you know, the workhouse – in a basket. They said as I must have floated here from foreign parts, over the sea, like Moses in his basket, but I never met Moses, so I dunno.

'Any road, skin and bone, I was. They said as they didn't think I'd live, but I did, in spite of them all doing their best to prevent it. Kept me small so as I'd be good for the chimbleys. And that's where they sent me, soon as they could get rid of me.'

'Your skin shines as if you were born under the sun, like the people of my country,' insisted the tiger. 'Was no token left with you, to tell who you were?'

Fly was about to shake her head, but then she stopped.

'There was just an old box,' she said. 'Just a rubbishy old metal box. With lines on it, like writing or pictures maybe, but they never learned me most of me letters, so I wouldn't know. It don't even open. It's still at Black Bill's. He took it off me when he got me from the workhouse.'

'We must get it back,' said the tiger. 'It may hold the secret of your royal birth.'

'Oh, that old baloney,' Fly snorted. She considered for a moment, torn between curiosity and the fear of Black Bill. She still didn't believe for one moment that she was a princess, and the thought of falling back into that man's clutches set her shivering again, but she was never going to admit for a moment, even to herself, that she was scared.

'You're on! It'll be a lark! We'll go tomorrow night!' She grinned.

As always, the promise of an adventure won.

CHAPTER 5

'What is the thing that follows you?'

Fly jolted awake. It was dawn and the tiger was back at his lookout post. Grubby grey light sulked beyond the open doorway; the moon had given up and gone to bed long ago, but the sun was in no hurry to rise and spend another day being smothered by smog.

It wasn't the way Fly was usually woken. There had been no boot in her back, no dawn chorus of curses. She couldn't remember when she'd last snoozled so snug, tucked up tight as a tick against the tiger's warm belly.

'What thing? Where? It ain't Black Bill, is it?' She scrambled to her feet and wriggled into her damp rags, putting the feather, which she had clutched all night, carefully back in the pocket. Her heart was thumping, as she peered past the tiger through the early-morning mist rolling in off the river. She could see nothing but the spikes of ships' masts and the dark swirling current in one direction, and the grey skyline of the city the other.

'You cannot see it?'

'There's nowt there.' Fly's sharp little chin set stubborn, in a face that nobody had ever loved enough to tell her was shaped like a heart. 'I can't see nuffin.'

'It has followed us since we left the menagerie. It comes after you, like a shadow. Have you never seen it?'

'Never.' Fly shook her head obstinately, but the tiger saw dread in her black eyes. His whiskers twitched. Was it the truth? Did she really not see it? Or did she just not want to see it?

'What is it then?' she demanded. 'Does it belong to Black Bill?' Her old master was still the worst thing she could imagine. Unlike the tiger, she had no inkling of the deeper evil to come.

'It is more powerful than anything that fool could conjure.' The tiger shook his head. 'All I know is that it does not have good intent towards you.

'It has no eyes and it has no nostrils, yet somehow it smells you out. I have heard of such things in my country. They call it a golem.'

Fly suppressed a shudder. Then, 'Can't you just eat it?' She was always on the lookout for a practical solution. 'Kill two birds with one stone, like.'

'I cannot eat evil.'

'No, I can see as that might disagree with your digestion.'

There was silence as the tiger gazed steadily out at whatever it was he could see.

'I will have to find a way to hide you from it,' he said, and he turned back inside.

'Didn't know as you was that colour,' Stick remarked, when he turned up at breakfast-time, as promised, with a sack full of dubious-smelling meat for the tiger and some apples for Fly. 'Never seen you not soot-black. It suits you!' Spud and Sparrow stayed down below, wobbling nervously from foot to foot like a couple of badly set jellies on a plate.

'Never been so clean.' Fly's face felt hot and she bit down on an apple. 'Not sure as it's healthy. But he's always washing his-self – and he gets in a fair old tweak if I don't.'

She didn't tell Stick about the moonlight swim. It felt like a piece of magic that might dissolve if too many people got to look at it. She hadn't told him she was a princess either, even though he was the closest she'd ever come to a brother, 'cos she knew he'd fall over laughing. And she didn't tell him about the golem, 'cos she didn't even want to think about that. But she did tell him about the plan to go back to Black Bill's, and he wasn't happy.

'You must be loose in the attic, Fly, going back there. What if he catches you? He'll give you a right walloping!'

'I left something there, Stick, and I wants it back. 'Sides, I'll sneak down his chimbley and he'll never know I was there!'

In the end Stick agreed they'd meet her at Black Bill's at midnight, when the evening's tumbling was done, because there was no way they were going to let her risk it on her own. Or, indeed, miss out on the chance of a lark.

Fly and the tiger spent the day sleeping in the safety of the old warehouse. Or at least Fly slept; the tiger was restless, getting up to pace to the doorway every few minutes before returning to lie next to her, watching over her as his mother had watched over him long ago, as a cub.

'Never had a snooze in the daytime afore,' Fly remarked when she woke up. 'I is like one of them la-di-da ladies what I used to drop in on, when they was partaking of an arternoon nap.'

At last it was dark outside. High tide had come and gone and it was time to leave for Black Bill's. The tiger peered out and Fly heard him give a low growl, as if he didn't like what he saw. She looked too, but still she saw nothing.

'Climb on my back,' the tiger grunted.

Fly hesitated. It still felt like a liberty too far to take a ride on the tiger.

'It don't seem right, mister,' she said. 'It's like old King Billy giving me a piggy-back down Pall Mall.' She snorted at the memory of the fossilised old bit of royalty she'd once seen bowling past the crowds in his golden carriage with not even a wave, holding a lace hankersniff to his nose to keep out the smell of his people. It was all she knew of what it meant to be a king. 'Mind you, he looked like he could hardly carry his crown, least of all me!' she scoffed.

But the tiger growled again and Fly knew better by now than to argue.

She laid one hand flat on his back and felt sparks fly up through her veins, like the bottled lightning back at the fair. 'Cripes, mister!' she whispered. 'What is you made of?'

She took a breath and cocked her leg over the tiger's long back. Then she swung herself up, settling in the dip behind his strong shoulders so she could hang on to fistfuls of his thick fur. But nothing could prepare her for the surge of power she felt when he launched himself from the doorway.

As he landed soundlessly in the soft mud, the tiger looked about again. She could have sworn he was purring, like a cat with its head stuck in a bowl of cream.

'Good,' he muttered. 'It is as I thought. It cannot see you when you are touching me.'

He leaped forwards, with a mighty bound. Fly had thought for a moment of giving the tiger a gee-up, like she'd seen the posh gents do to their horses when they were riding down Rotten Row. But that moment didn't last long. There was no way she could have controlled the wild gallop that followed. This was no royal progress with the princess sitting tall and proud and waving graciously at her subjects. The best Fly could do was to cling on and gasp out directions to Black Bill's.

Most of the city was sleeping, and those who were abroad were so dumb-flustered with drink that she hardly needed to befuddle their brains to stop them seeing a tiger streaking past. *Any road, the gin's probably got them seeing pink elephants, so a tiger won't be no surprise,* she thought.

The city's bells were striking midnight, each a few moments apart, like they were arguing about the time, when Fly and the tiger arrived at the squalid street where Black Bill and his wife lived. The couple had the downstairs rooms in a little two-up, two-down they shared with another sweep and his missus. Only another sweep could have put up with the stench and the dirt. The place stank of soot and was as black as a coal mine inside, but if nobody washed, nobody noticed. Now she was clean, Fly's own nose was wrinkling as much as the tiger's.

Opposite Black Bill's, Stick's long, thin body was propped up in his usual pose – one foot back against the wall, teeth clamped on the unlit pipe. He pushed himself upright and Spud and Sparrow melted out of the shadows to join them. Sparrow was dabs at lurking in the shadows and watching houses without being seen, thanks to his apprenticeship to the house-breaker.

'He's home,' said Sparrow.

'Half-seas over,' added Stick.

Fly nodded. 'He says he drinks to wash the soot down, stops it rotting his insides.'

'Him and his missus was knocking seven bells out of each other, but it's all quiet now,' Sparrow told her.

'Bit of luck, they've knocked each other out,' Spud muttered.

'I've brought some rope, so as I can pull you out if you gets into trouble,' said Stick, who'd been thinking through the plan ever since Fly told him she was going down the chimney. 'I'll come up top with you and Spud, and Sparrow can keep watch down here.'

Fly started to get off the tiger's back, but he growled a low growl. 'Stay! If you stop touching me, the golem will find you.'

So she clung on to his shoulders as he leaped effortlessly to the roof. Stick scrambled up the drainpipe behind them.

The moonlight was more ragged than the night before, but it escaped from the clouds now and the shining roofs of London stretched away in silver waves like an ocean. The rooftops were Fly's world, and she slid confidently off the tiger's back and perched on the chimney stack.

'You must be quick before it smells you out!' The tiger hung his head and paws over the gutter, and peered down into the shadows of the street below.

'Here,' said Stick, handing her the rope and tying one end round his waist. 'Tie this round you – just give it a tug if you needs to come back up sharpish. If I needs to warn you about something, I'll give it two tugs.'

Fly nodded and swallowed hard. After her escape from Black Bill, she hadn't reckoned on going down any more chimneys, and this was a narrow one – the sort she woke up sweating about in her nightmares. But at least it wasn't Black Bill pushing her down there this time.

'Go! Before it finds you!' The tiger growled another low growl, impatient now.

Fly dangled her legs down and felt the soot-thick space close around her like a brick coffin. She braced her hands and feet and edged her way down, breathing shallow all the way. The trick was to keep your lungs as empty as possible without waking up dead.

'Don't bring your knees too high, girl,' she muttered, remembering all the sweeplings she knew who'd never lived to tell the tale.

More than half-way down, and she was getting close to Black Bill's kitchen. She stopped and listened. All quiet, but for snores from the bedroom. Where had the old skinflint stowed her box? He kept the stuff she nicked for him under his bed, but she'd never seen her box there. Mind you, he'd larruped her every time she'd tried to sneak a look, so she couldn't be sure.

She was about to drop down into the fireplace when she felt two strong tugs on the rope. Stick's warning sign. She braced herself against the brickwork.

It was then that the knocking started, on the door.

Whoever that is, they is not popping round for tea, thought Fly. These weren't your polite sort of knocks. These sounded like blows from a heavy stick. *Croopus! They'd have a dead man sitting up in his grave with that rumpus!*

The snores from the bedroom stopped. Another pounding at the door. Black Bill's stumbling steps, cursing as he lifted the latch. 'Who the devil . . .?'

A new voice spoke. 'You have lost her!'

It was a man's voice, a high, syrup-sweet whine with an underlying hiss. If a snake could speak, this was how it would sound. Fly couldn't get any picture in her head of what such a man would look like, but his voice was enough to seep fear into her soul. And Fly didn't scare easy.

'No, my lord,' stammered Black Bill.

It sounded like fear had betwaddled his few wits. Fly had never heard Bill frightened before, but she wasn't enjoying it as much as she might have done normal-times, because she was as scared as he was.

'You were well rewarded for keeping the girl close. Yet I am told she is gone. Where is she?'

The voice was quiet, but deadly. *Bust me!* thought Fly. *Whoever that cove is, he don't even need to shout to scare a person into convulsions.*

Below, Bill's battle-axe of a wife came storming out of the bedroom. 'Can't good God-fearing folks get a night's sleep round here?'

Working herself up into a right humdinger! Fly allowed herself a grin because, for once, she was out of range for a beating.

Bill's wife was still going. 'It ain't right—' but then she let out a squawk of terror, like a scalded hen. 'Pardon me, my lord.' Her footsteps scuttled back into the bedroom and the door slammed behind her. Black Bill was on his own.

'Where is the girl?' the voice insisted.

Fly heard Black Bill stumble, like he was backing away from someone who just kept coming. Then came a thud against the wall. He had clearly run out of room to get away.

'I'll soon find her!' The words were struggling to get out of Bill's throat, as if someone had a hand gripped tight about his windpipe. 'She'll be hanging round with that gang of gutterlings – that's where she goes of an evening,' he gasped. 'I'll find her tomorrow and give her what for.'

'Tomorrow may be too late . . . I am told she has found a powerful friend.'

Now would have been the time to go. One tug of the rope and Stick would pull her up to safety. But for a girl who prided herself on always knowing the quickest way out, something was stopping her from thinking straight. Something was starting to exert its evil over her, and she could no more move than she could have danced a jig in that chimney.

A silence. Then came a whisper, hardly heard, like the scuttering of a spider. Not a human voice but something else. The sudden dread Fly was feeling told her that it was the thing the tiger had warned her about. The golem was down there in the room. It had smelled her out.

And then a high tinkling laugh of pure evil. 'Ha! I am told we have found what we were looking for. The girl has come to us!'

And, quick as lightning, a fat silk-clad arm slid up the chimney and a plump brown hand, bristling with rings, fastened like a vice around Fly's ankle. Fly's arms flailed behind her as she tried to catch hold of the rope, and knocked something loose from a gap in the bricks. It was her metal box. It must have been stowed up the chimney for safekeeping by Black Bill.

'Tarnation!' Fly cursed as the box fell into the cold ashes. 'Stick!' Her hand finally found the rope and she tugged hard.

Stick must have felt the sudden pull, because the rope tightened like a noose around her waist and for a wild moment of hope she believed he would win the tug of war over her body. But then there was a glint of a blade and the rope went slack around her. Then she saw nothing more, as she was yanked down into the room and everything went dark.

CHAPTER 6

Stick fell back from the chimney stack as the rope suddenly gave way. He would have rolled right off the roof if the tiger hadn't stopped him with a deft paw.

'The golem smelled her out,' the tiger growled. 'I should not have let her go alone.'

Stick had no notion what the tiger was saying – all he heard was the growl. But in the street below he could see a cursing and kicking sackful of Fly being carried out under the arm of a tall thin man. The man, who wore black silks which glistened like oil in the gas-light, bundled her through the door of a waiting carriage.

As the thin man leaped up to the driver's seat and seized the reins, a second man followed him out of the house, draped in silks as bright as the other man's were dark. He had the rolling gait of a very fat man, but he stepped as lightly as a dancer, on tiny feet that looked like he'd stolen them from a dead child.

The fat man climbed into the black carriage and was pulling down the blinds, when Black Bill came running out after him and grabbed hold of the carriage door.

'My lord, you said as there'd be something for the missus and me, a reward, if we kept her close . . .'

'Cripes! He's more of a fool than Fly said!' muttered Stick, watching from the roof. The evil in the fat man's face, as he glared back at Bill through the carriage window, made Stick shiver.

'But you failed, you fool,' the fat man hissed. 'You are lucky I'm leaving you alive. Forget all you know of the girl, and all you know of me, or it will be the worse for you. You saw nothing.' He rapped the roof of the carriage with his metal-tipped stick. 'Drive on!'

The driver's whip flicked back and cut Black Bill across the face, leaving him bleeding and cursing as the horses sprang forward and away.

'What now?' Stick asked the tiger. But the tiger was already gone. Stick turned to look at the fast-disappearing carriage, and caught the gleam of stripes in the moonlight as the tiger bounded after his princess.

'What now?' Stick asked again, this time to Spud and Sparrow, after he'd slid down the drainpipe. 'We've lost her. I told her as she shouldn't come back.'

'Who was that cove?' asked Spud. 'He was a right shavey customer! What's he want with Fly?'

Stick shrugged. 'I dunno, but I don't like it. How is we going to find her now?'

'I has seen him afore, when I were sweeping the crossings.' Spud looked like he had seen a ghost. 'I'd know that coat of harms on them carriage doors anywhere . . . it's got a picture of two jumbos all trussed up in chains.'

He shook his head in a way that didn't bode well for Fly. 'I has seen that stick of his afore, too. He beat one of the crossing-sweepers over the head with it, just 'cos little Jim asked for a penny for clearing the crossing for him.' Spud shivered. 'He was never the same arterwards, little Jim. Croaked it, he did, in the hospital, two weeks later.'

Nobody said anything for a bit, then: 'We'll put the word out, on the crossings, then,' said Stick. 'Sweepers will soon find her. They loves Fly.'

'We all loves Fly,' Sparrow said quietly, to nobody in particular.

So the word went out and spread like lightning around the streets of London. By noon, when the toffs strolled out to take the air and the gossip over a spot of lunch, there wasn't a crossing-sweeper in the city who wasn't on the lookout for a black coach bearing a coat of arms with two elephants tied up in chains.

'He's a havey-cavey sort, greasy as a lump of lard, and he's got our Fly,' went the word. Everyone knew Fly, whose stories were always bang-up slumdingers, and who always prigged the best grub – and what's more, wasn't above sharing it, too. Fly was one of their own, and no dicey cove was going to snaffle her on their watch.

Most days the tumblers slept late, after cartwheeling for the toffs until midnight, but today the three of them were already perched outside a church in the heart of the city. The churchwarden had tried to shoo them off with his broom, but they kept settling back down like a flock of tattered starlings as soon as he'd turned away. So he gave up and left them there receiving a constant stream of gutter-boys and gutter-girls, like kings of a very shabby court. From the steps, their network of informants stretched out in a spider's web across London.

But none of their news was good. The tales they heard about the fat man were all as bad, or worse, than the story

Spud had told the night before. Acts of casual cruelty . . .
beatings handed out for the slightest offence . . . gutterlings,
not quick enough on their feet, getting trapped beneath his
carriage wheels and left for dead. And the crushers doing
nothing, either for fear or because they were in his pay.
They called themselves policemen but all they cared about
were the toffs.

What was missing was any clue about where this monster
lived . . . and until he ventured out of his house again, even
the sweepers couldn't tell them where Fly had been taken.

CHAPTER 7

A king, whose skin gleams like burnished copper, sits tall and proud in robes that shimmer like the yellow sun.

He is suspended in a golden cage, and his tears fall fast into the sacred river far below.

His only food is figs, fed to him through the bars by golden monkeys that leap lightly from the tall trees, which bend to shield him from the burning sun.

His only drink is sweet water dripped from the beaks of scarlet hummingbirds that hover about his cage.

His heart is broken, and, as he weeps, he cries out:

'Oh, my lost children!

'Oh, my poor people!

'Oh, my poor creatures!

'Brother, have pity!'
But nobody hears his cries.

Fly woke with a name on her lips that she'd never said before and didn't even know she knew, and as fast as she woke, the name was gone, along with the dream.

But she might as well have still been dreaming, for the strangeness of what met her eyes when they opened.

'Blimey, what a bang-up joint!'

She tried to sit up but her head was swimming and her mouth was full of a taste so sweet it was making her gag, so she lay back down and closed her eyes while she tried to work out where she was and how she had got here.

She was lying on sheets of the finest satin, which whispered to her to close her eyes and dream again, but what was left of the old Fly in her poppy-drugged head was telling her she must get up and fight or she might just sleep for ever.

Just take it slow, girl, she thought.

She opened her eyes and swallowed hard to keep from being sick, although her belly couldn't remember when it had last eaten.

'So there's nowt in there to spoil those naffy sheets, any road,' she said out loud, and hearing her own voice was a good start. *At least there's someone here I knows,* she thought.

There was pink shiny stuff everywhere she looked. It took her a bit to work out that she was in a four-poster bed draped with the same palest-pink satin as the sheets.

'Looks like I has been swallowed by a whale . . .' said Fly, out loud again, for company, and to keep herself awake, because the poppy syrup she had been given was still whispering to her to return to her dreams.

'Sit up, Fly,' she told herself, to shut out the poppy syrup's sweet call, and she slowly levered herself on to her elbows and peered out through the curtains.

She'd never seen a room like this, even when Bill had her nicking gee-gaws from the grandest houses. There were deep velvet cushions scattered over the floor, and the walls were hung with tapestries of the richest crimsons and scarlets. The tapestries mostly showed animals being hunted and killed, and the scarlet was mostly the blood of dying animals.

Cor! Love a lily-white duck! These coves must be precious fond of killing things, thought Fly.

It was the tapestry opposite the bed that brought up what little there was in her stomach and left her retching into a pink pillow. It was an image of a tiger snarling, defiant to death, a spear thrust deep into its throat.

'It ain't you, it ain't you!' she whispered into the pillow, saying it over and over to make it true. 'I won't never let them do that to you!'

At last she sat up, keeping her eyes turned away from the tapestry. *What kind of devil wants to wake up to that every morning?*

Fly had nothing but the haziest memory of what had happened after she had been yanked out of the chimney. She'd only got a brief glimpse of the fat man who had seized her and stuffed her, kicking, into a sack. It was probably better she didn't remember.

The room was hot and airless, but Fly was shivering. Her rags had been replaced by a silk nightdress of the same sickly pink as the sheets.

'Blimey, I looks like a blancmange!'

She slipped her legs from under the sheets, the silky stuff tugging at her limbs until it finally yielded and let her go, and she slid her feet to the ground. It didn't feel like any floor Fly had ever trodden; her toes sank into a carpet so thick she lost sight of them under the sea of crimson.

'Where you gone?' she called down to them, and they

wriggled to tell her they were still there. 'Talking to your toes, Fly,' she said sternly. 'That ain't a good sign.'

There was nothing about any of this that felt real. This room had none of the hard edges of Fly's world. It was soft and rich and muffled in luxury. Fly felt as if she was being suffocated like a grub in a silk cocoon and nobody would hear her, no matter how loud she screamed.

Except she had been heard.

In the silence, her ears picked up the same scuttling whisper that had filled her with dread when she was hiding in the chimney. The golem was outside the door, and it knew that she was awake.

Fly tried to prepare herself for what was on the other side of the door. She wriggled quickly out of the nightgown but her rags were nowhere to be seen.

'Drabbit it! Where's me feather?' she muttered, with a pang of loss.

A pair of soft gathered trousers and a long, richly embroidered shift had been laid out on the bed, so she slipped them on instead.

'I looks like a kipper!' Orange wasn't the sort of colour a gutterling would choose to slip through the streets unnoticed.

She ignored the embroidered slippers. She didn't rightly know if it was possible for her feet to run in shoes, never having worn any, and running was what she planned to do the moment the door opened. Her plan was to put the stares on the golem, and be gone.

Except it didn't work out that way.

The door opened, but the light beyond was blocked by the immense bulk of the fat man. Swathed in robes so brilliant it looked like he'd crushed birds of paradise to steal their colours, he swept into the room on silent, slippered feet, sending Fly stumbling back towards the bed. Just the sound of his voice had been enough to frighten her the night before; the sight of him destroyed any dream of running away.

Above the draped robes, the fat man's many chins hung down below a face that settled in flabby folds underneath a pair of bulging brown eyes. A very small, perfectly trimmed, dart-shaped beard clung to the bottom chin, like the forked tongue of a snake, but otherwise he was completely hairless. He was so ugly he took Fly's breath away.

He looks like a toad what's eaten all the other toads, and now it's looking around for something else to snack on, she thought.

He had the same dark skin as Fly, but his face was dull and bloated and on his bald head was perched a kind of flattened mop cap that put Fly in mind of a muffin. On a normal day, out on the street, she and the tumblers would have fallen over laughing at the absurdity of that hat. But she didn't need to have heard Spud's story about little Jim the crossing-sweeper to tell her that this man was not someone to be laughed at.

'So, our little guttersnipe is awake at last.'

The fat man placed a hand on Fly's head and the weight felt like it would crush all the hope from her heart. He paused and inclined his head to one side. There it was, that whisper again, like he was carrying on a constant conversation with something evil sitting on his shoulder. She still couldn't see it, but the dread deepened, now the tiger had told her what was there.

Fly gave herself a shake. There was a sweet smell hanging about the fat man that oozed into her head and made her want to vomit again. She tried to summon the strength to put the stares on him, but she might as well have tried to bewitch a mountain.

'Your little tricks don't work on me, I'm afraid, my dear child.' The fat man's tinkling laugh could have soured milk. 'It takes deeper magic than you possess, with your untrained mind, to fool a master.'

She shook his hand off her head and stood back in a last desperate show of defiance. She squared her shoulders.

'You got something of mine, mister, what you took from Black Bill's last night. Fair's fair, I wants it back, and then I'll be gone, if it's all the same to you.'

The fat man smiled, and the folds of his flesh rippled and rearranged themselves around his face. 'You are impertinent, child. You must understand that you belong to me now. But we will have a little chat over tea. First you must be washed. You are dirtying my carpets.'

With that he turned and sailed away down a flight of gleaming white marble stairs, his loose robes billowing about him.

After he had gone, Fly just stood there, staring after him, dazed and befuddled. She knew that she should run, she knew that she should try to escape, but her instincts were betwaddled by the power of the fat man and the lingering effects of the poppy syrup.

She felt a light touch on her arm and jumped. 'Bust me!'

A girl dressed in black, not much older than she was, had appeared from nowhere. She had the same dark skin and black hair as Fly, but her hair swung long down her back while Fly's was as short and stiff as a cockatoo's crest.

'What you doing, creeping up on a person like that?' protested Fly. 'You scared the be-jeepers out of me!'

The girl said nothing. She beckoned and led Fly back into the bedroom and then into a smaller room. It was tiled in white and contained a large roll-top bath which was full to the brim with steaming, perfumed water. She pointed to tell Fly she was to get in.

'Cripes! More washing!' But she didn't have much choice, and the girl was still saying nothing.

'Cat got your tongue?' snapped Fly, because the girl's silence was beginning to irritate her.

She still did not respond.

Fly had heard about baths, like she'd heard about heaven, but she'd never been in one. She sank gingerly into the hot water.

'Ain't I the dandy!' she whispered in wonder.

As always, her first thought was how she would spin this story tonight on the street. But then she shivered in spite of the heat and remembered that she didn't rightly know where she would be tonight, because it didn't look like the fat man was planning to let her go any time soon. *It's like being in chokey, even if it's chokey what's padded with silk,* she thought.

The girl still said nothing, but pointed shyly to a bar of soap and mimed for Fly to rub it on her arms. While Fly washed, the girl picked up the orange clothes Fly had briefly worn and wrinkled her nose at the soot. She went out and came back with a clean set, this time in a turquoise blue.

'Why is I here?' Fly asked, as she stepped out of the bath and wrapped herself in thick, soft towels. But the girl just looked frightened and shook her head.

Fly looked at the new set of clothes. All these clothes fitted like they'd been made for her. *It's like they was waiting for me,* she thought. It wasn't a comfortable thought.

'Where's my togs?' she demanded. The girl looked puzzled. 'My kecks . . . trousers. There's something in the pocket I really need . . .'

The girl looked uncertain.

'Please . . .' Fly wasn't used to begging for favours, but she really wanted the scarlet feather. It felt important, without knowing why.

The girl whisked away again. When she came back her nose was even more wrinkled, but she was holding out Fly's torn and filthy trousers. She watched as Fly pulled out the scarlet feather and Fly heard her gasp, as if she had seen the birds it had come from, once, in another place. It was the first sound she'd heard the girl make.

'You been struck dumb or something?' she demanded impatiently, pulling on the new set of clothes and putting the feather carefully in a pocket.

The girl looked frightened again and shook her head.

'Don't be daffy – he can't hear us. What's your name?'

The girl looked behind her nervously. Then she seemed to make a decision. She opened her mouth and pointed at the place where her tongue should be. There was nothing there.

Fly turned away quickly, swallowing down a surge of nausea. What sort of monster would have cut out this girl's tongue? She finished dressing, feeling the silence pressing in on her.

Where was her tiger? For that was how she thought of him now. *Her* tiger. Had he escaped into the night? Her heart ached. She wanted to sink her fingers into his thick coat and feel the strength of him pacing beside her. How could he return to his home now, without her help?

Like the rest of the house, the drawing room was shuttered to keep out the sun, and there was no fire nor candles burning.

It was so dark and quiet in the room, it was like she had been swallowed by a snake. But even though she couldn't see much, Fly knew that there was something in there waiting for her.

She'd been brought down to the drawing room by the thin black-robed manservant who had shoved her into the carriage the night before – although Fly had no memory of him. As he led her down the gleaming marble staircase and across the hall, she saw a golden cage standing empty. The door to the cage was open, as if it was waiting for something to be locked behind its bars.

The manservant had ushered her into the drawing room and left her there, closing the door behind him. Fly's slippered feet sank into the deep carpet; the girl had oiled the hard skin on her soles and encased them in the embroidered silk slippers.

Blimey, thought Fly. *It ain't half quiet.* There was not a sound, yet she had seen plenty of servants gliding around the house. *Has they all lost their tongues, like that girl?* Fly was still fighting down the nausea. *Best not lob your groats on this carpet, girl – can't see as that would go down too well with His Nibs.*

There was a golden clock encrusted with emeralds and sapphires on the sideboard. But it too was silent. *Even the clocks don't dare tick*, thought Fly. It made her want to shout out all the many bad words she knew, but her courage was failing her, like everything else that made her Fly.

Yet there was still something calling to her in this room, and so she took a step further in.

There it was, on a low table. Her old, tarnished metal box, covered in symbols and letters that she couldn't understand. She kneeled beside the table to look more closely. As she remembered, there was no visible join between lid and box. She hesitated to touch it; something told her that once she picked it up this time, there would be no escaping from this adventure. No way back to the Fly of the streets.

On the instant that it felt her hands around it, the box fell open into two perfect halves, as if it had been waiting for this moment, as if it had been waiting for her to be ready. Inside, on a black velvet cushion, glowed a ruby the size of a child's heart. A flame flickered deep inside it, like it was pleased to see her. She felt as though it was whispering to her, telling her that she could do anything, as long as she held it in her hands.

'That is a thing of great beauty that you are holding.'

The fat man had slid into the room without her hearing and was gazing greedily at the ruby, as if he wanted to gobble it down.

'Its name is *Nga Ran*, or Heart of the Tiger,' he went on. 'It has been lost for many years.' But the flame inside the ruby had died instantly at the sound of his voice, and something like fear now replaced the greed in his eyes.

The ruby does not work for him. Fly tucked that thought away.

The fat man's silk-clad arm slithered out to seize it, but Fly snapped the box shut; the join was instantly invisible. He snatched it from her and shook it, but the halves stayed shut.

'How did you open it?' he demanded.

Fly shrugged. 'I dunno. It never opened before.'

The fat man gave a little hiss of contempt and frustration. 'The little fool has powers she does not comprehend,' he muttered. 'How did you come by it?'

''Tis mine,' Fly stated, knowing it was true. 'It were left with me, in my basket, at the workhouse.'

'How did it come there?' He turned to stare accusingly at his manservant, who had come back in silently behind him. Fly couldn't see his face in the shadows. She shrugged.

'And why does it open only for you?'

Fly shrugged again, because it seemed to annoy him, and he gave another little hiss and looked like he wanted to slap her. But then he smoothed the frowns from his flabby face.

'No matter,' he said briskly. 'It was yours, but now you are mine, so the ruby is mine also.'

Taking the box, he stepped lightly towards the fireplace. At a gesture of his ring-encrusted hand, an opening appeared in the wall.

Cor, love-a-lily-white-duck! Fly's eyes widened at the pile of gold inside. *You could buy every pie in London with all that, and still have enough to buy plum duff for pudding!*

The fat man shut her treasure away with another waft of his hand. 'And now, tea-time, I think.'

Servants, all dressed in black silks and all as silent as the girl, filed in carrying tea things on silver trays. There was not the slightest chink of china or clink of cutlery as the meal was laid out, and then they were gone, leaving Fly with the fat man.

Lawks, what's the matter with them all? They all needs a good shake! She was finding it increasingly difficult to keep up her normal chatter with herself as the stifling atmosphere, heavy with evil, pressed in on her.

'I disposed of their tongues when they came here, to stop their incessant chattering,' the fat man said. It was as if she had spoken out loud. As if he could hear her thoughts. 'If they cannot talk, they cannot plot against me. Only Dalit kept his tongue. It is useful to me to have one servant who can speak.'

He nodded at the thin manservant, as still as a statue at the back of the room.

Fly looked round. The room was full of cases containing exotic stuffed animals with glass eyes that stared at her like they were accusing her of some crime. As if it was *her* fault they were there, instead of roaming free. When she looked back at the fat man, he was staring at her too, like she was another small animal he was contemplating stuffing and adding to his collection.

'Shall I be mother?' With a grotesquely girlish simper, he crooked his little finger and poured a golden liquid into Fly's cup, then poured a cup for himself from a different teapot.

'Eat! Drink!' He swept a pudgy hand towards the table, to show Fly that she should help herself. He popped a tiny cake into his own cavernous mouth and crushed it between sharp, little white teeth that looked like a row of tombstones.

Fly hesitated. The sweetness of the smells that rose from her cup and from the delicacies laid out in front of her were reminding her of the previous night and making her nauseous again. But her stomach was rumbling, and she'd never *seen* so much food, let alone eaten it, without running the risk of getting locked up. In the end, hunger won.

'I can hear you eating,' the fat man said, with distaste.

She made an effort to stuff the food in more quietly, but it wasn't easy when you were that hungry. When it came to food, it had to be admitted that Fly had the manners of a hedge-fish.

She squinted at him from beneath lowered eyelids. Normally she had a knack for working out what made someone tick, and how to get round them, but as she sipped the sweet golden tea, understanding what he was up to seemed to matter less and less.

Difficult to tell what a cove is thinking when he's got a face like cold stew and dumplings, she thought, sleepily.

At last, without any signal that she noticed, the servants reappeared and took everything soundlessly away. Fly had never been one to follow orders before, but now she found herself waiting to be told what to do next.

A scuttling whisper at the fat man's shoulder. Even through her daze it made Fly shudder.

'I am told you have a friend who is hiding in my shrubbery,' he said smoothly. 'I would very much like to meet him. Go and call him in.'

Fly's black eyes, normally alight with the latest lark, gazed dully back at him. There was some part of her that knew what she was about to do was deeply wrong, but the sweet stuff he had slipped into her golden tea had made her forget why it mattered.

'The door, Dalit!' the fat man ordered.

His manservant pulled back the shutters that covered the French windows. Fly stepped out into a garden as lush and luxuriant as a jungle.

'Tiger!' she called, and the great beast emerged from where he had been waiting for her in the bushes. His stripes gleamed in the shadows as he padded soundlessly towards her. Then he paused and waited, gazing at Fly. So quiet. So still. He knew what was waiting for him. He knew he was about to lose his freedom once more.

There was no surprise, just infinite hurt in the tiger's golden eyes as he looked at Fly, while the servants in black silk threw nets over him and dragged him to the ground.

Fly had betrayed her tiger.

CHAPTER 8

'I swear, it were our Fly, right enough, but she don't look like our Fly no more . . .'

'She were done up all dandy, in posh togs, and her hair – you know how her hair always sticks up like a bottlebrush . . . it were all flat and shiny against her head . . .'

'And she looked out the windy of the trot-box, and she looked straight at me, but she never saw me . . . it were like she were asleep with her eyes open.'

A council of war was being held, in the old warehouse that was still creakily arguing with itself over whether or not to give up and tumble into the Thames. It was a full three days since Fly and the tiger had vanished, but this was the first sighting the sweepers had to report.

Stick, Spud and Sparrow had called a meeting of mudlarks, crossing-sweepers and tumblers, all old friends of Fly's. A rich aroma of river-mud and street-dirt and sweat rose from their never-washed bodies. And the rats, who had never really gone away, but had been hiding under the floorboards, crept out to relish the smell in the hope of nibbling on an unwary toe.

'Was that fat cove with her?' demanded Spud. He wasn't going to forget that man and what he'd done to little Jimmy in a hurry.

Squinty, the lanky, cross-eyed sweeper who had spoken first, nodded. 'He was sitting next to her, and when he saw me looking at Fly, he leaned over and pulled down the blind, sharpish-like.'

'But it were the right carriage and no mistake,' insisted the other sweeper, who was known as Bandy on account of his legs. Unlike Squinty's eyes, Bandy's knees were intent on getting as far away from each other as possible. 'With that coat of harms with them poor trussed-up jumbos on the doors. They looks right miserable, them jumbos.'

'We has seen that trot-box down by the docks, often-times . . .' chimed in one of the mudlarks. Teresa – or Tree – spent her days grubbing around in the filthy mud of the Thames, never giving up hope of finding a fortune flushed out with the sewage.

'Is he that cove what comes to meet that shavey captain when his ship comes in from foreign parts?' asked her sister Cecily – Cess for short.

'That's the one.' Tree nodded. 'The ship with all them big crates what makes all them noises, like souls being tortured in Hell . . .' Tree and her sister knew all about Hell. They'd grown up being threatened daily with damnation by the nuns at the orphanage, who tried to beat some religion into them until their legs grew long enough to run away. The nuns also gave them their saints' names, which soon got translated into something more suitable for the streets. The pair of them were so pale and skinny, it was only a thick coating of mud that made them visible.

'I remember!' said Cess. 'It were one of them crates what got left open, when that tiger got out and tried to eat that little tyke . . . there were a right to-do . . .'

'And then the fat cove with the carriage beat the tiger over the head with his stick, and then they dragged it back in the crate and he took it away . . .' Tree finished. The sisters always liked to share out stories between them, so each of them got their fair share.

'That were Fly's tiger!' cried Sparrow. The rest of the council of war looked startled. The tumblers hadn't mentioned the tiger, for fear it might make them less inclined to look for Fly.

'So what was the fat man doing at the docks, talking to a ship's captain?' Stick asked. If Fly had been there, she would have recognised that look on Stick's whip-smart face, as he began to bring all the threads together. 'And what does he want with our Fly?'

'We needs to follow that trot-box,' said Spud.

'Already done,' replied Bandy. 'We been watching. We knows where she is. Come with us.'

After three days of being drugged with poppy syrup, there wasn't much left of the Fly who danced over rooftops and put the stares on half of London and told stories that kept the gutterlings hanging on her every word past midnight. She'd given up the fight against the fat man's dark magic, which seemed so much stronger than her own little talent for unseeing.

She drifted about the silent house on her silk-shod feet, eating when she was told to eat and drinking more and more of the golden tea, which she now craved even before she was told to drink. She'd fallen into the habit of silence that the fat man imposed on everyone in that house. She didn't even talk to herself out loud any more.

But in fact, there was a lot going on inside Fly's head. She was busy dreaming, even while she was awake. The dreams, which the fat man knew nothing of, and could not control, became more and more vivid – dreams of a king calling out for his lost children, and weeping for the people and the animals of his stolen kingdom. That kingdom was an impossibly beautiful place, a land beyond imagining, nothing like the gutters Fly knew so well.

The poppy syrup had brought back memories from before the age of remembering, memories she didn't know she had, of milk-white domes translucent beneath cloudless blue skies, of stately palaces and pleasure gardens bright with exotic blooms. Memories of a land of green-robed hills and snow-topped mountains, with crystal waterfalls cascading into a sacred river, running down to an ink-dark sea. And memories of the sanctuary of a mother's lap. And of having been loved once. The old Fly would have dismissed these memories as a load of gammon, but for now they were a lot more fun than remembering that she had betrayed her tiger.

The tiger was behind bars once more, locked up in the golden cage that had been waiting for him in the hall. The fat man brought visitors to gawp at him, but the tiger just skulked stubbornly in the shadows. His shimmering coat was dimmed, as if the black stripes were swallowing up the gold.

'Show us your teeth, damn you!' spat the fat man, and he poked him with his metal-tipped stick.

Only then did the terrified visitors get a glimpse of the tiger's power, as he leaped, snarling, at the bars, and they scurried, terrified, for the door.

It was Fly that the tiger was watching for. When at last she came downstairs and drifted past in her poppy-haze, he padded to the front of the cage, but she wouldn't look at him.

'Princess . . .' He growled deep in his chest, as he smelled the sweetness of the poppy syrup on her skin. But it wasn't just the poppy syrup. The tiger could also see the shadow of the thing, dark as smoke, which hung about her everywhere she went, though she still did not see it.

'That thing is still stalking her,' he rumbled, and let out a bit of a roar, to see what would happen. He grinned as the golem squeaked and scuttled into a dark corner. 'It fears me. That is something.'

Fly turned to look when he roared, as if she was puzzled about something she half-remembered, but then looked away.

Still there, somewhere, the tiger thought.

But then the fat man appeared from the drawing room and brought the metal-tipped stick crashing down on the bars of the cage and the tiger withdrew to the shadows.

Fly looked on, saying nothing. But when the fat man called Dalit to bring round his carriage and indicated that Fly should join him, the tiger saw her look back at him from the door, as if she was trying to remember something, and the corners of his black lips curled once more into a grin.

It was on this trip in the carriage that Fly had been spotted by the crossing-sweepers and from that moment, everywhere the carriage went, a crossing-sweeper was attached to the back like a limpet, unbeknown to the fat man and his servant. They took it in turns to hop on and hop off, as they crossed each other's territory, whispering 'Tell Stick and the tumblers!' at every stop.

When the carriage stopped, even in her dazed state, Fly dimly recognised where she was. It was the place where all this had started. The menagerie.

The fat man got out and rapped on the door with his metal-tipped stick. The old guard opened up smartish this time; it was too early in the day for the gin to have got the better of his trousers. The fat man swept in, and Fly was ushered in after him by Dalit. They made a kind of sandwich, with Fly as the filling, and the crossing-sweeper who was on lookout could see there was no chance of rescuing her. He ran off to send a message to the others.

Inside the dimly lit menagerie, there was an uneasy stirring as the sickening scent of the fat man reached the beasts in their cages. They knew this man, and they knew all about his cruelty. It was him that had brought them here from the docks, after that long journey over the sea.

'Wake up, you lazy creatures!' he hissed as he strode from cage to cage, rattling his stick along the bars so even the lions retreated to the back, snarling but impotent. 'You need to look your best for my buyers!'

'Turn the water on them,' he snapped at the guard, who was slopping around after him. 'Nobody's going to want to buy this pile of moth-eaten fur rugs!'

Fly looked up. The colours of the birds above the net seemed dimmer than before. The floor was thick with feathers that reminded her vaguely about a promise: *'Her majesty will come back . . . she will not forget you . . .'* Whose voice was that?

The old guard hurried to fill buckets and started sloshing cold water into the cages. The largest elephant, who still had a bit of spirit left, squirted the water back through the bars, soaking the bright silks of the fat man's robes, until the stick came crashing down on its trunk and the huge beast cowered like a kitten against the wall.

There was a rap on the door, and Dalit glided over to open it. A toff in a tall hat, with a mean face framed by ginger whiskers like a fox, stalked in with a plump lady, fluffed up like a chicken, on his arm. She wore a dress of sprigged muslin over an abundance of petticoats, which caused some difficulty at the door, but eventually, with the help of Dalit and the guard, she was tugged through sideways like a ship being piloted into harbour.

Negotiations started after the petticoats had been settled and the men had bowed and shaken hands. The toffs toured the cages and inspected the wares; the fat man put a price on the head of each animal, while they tried to barter him down.

Like a fishmonger haggling over a barrow-load of bloaters, a voice remarked, somewhere in Fly's head.

'These beasts are all very well, my good man,' his foxy lordship whined, 'but we are looking for something rather special, something that will set tongues wagging at court. Something to please the king. Something with a bit of a roar, maybe?' He peered doubtfully at the damp lions, sulking soggily in the back of their cages.

Her ladyship the chicken looked distinctly nervous at the mention of roaring. 'But perhaps they could just roar at weekends, my love, when we have guests?'

'I have the very thing, my lord,' the fat man assured him. 'A remarkable beast, a tiger so magnificent that I keep it caged in my own home. But how much more impressed your guests will be, if you take the complete set?'

Like a fancy dinner service, with a silver tea-pot thrown in for good measure, muttered the voice in Fly's head.

At last the deal was done, with the birds added as a sweetener on top. 'The animals will be yours in four days' time, my lord. My man will arrange the transport.' The fat man sounded delighted with his deal.

All this time Fly appeared to see and hear nothing. She was ushered back to the carriage, but the beating of those wings against the glass roof felt like a drumbeat inside her head.

As she climbed in, she heard the manservant, Dalit, behind her.

'What are your plans for the girl, my lord?' He made no attempt to keep his voice down in front of her, as he handed his master in with a bow.

That servant cove is so oily you could fry a flounder with him, muttered the voice in Fly's head.

'We wait,' the fat man snapped. 'I have written to her uncle to find out what he wants done with her. Until I hear from him, we keep her close.'

He paused. 'By the by, Dalit, how came the ruby in the girl's possession? Her uncle has been seeking the *Nga Ran* for many years – he and his brother went to war with one another over that ruby – only for it to disappear on the day of his coronation! He only keeps his brother alive because he thinks one day he will tell him where the ruby is.'

The fat man's toad-eyes narrowed as he looked hard at Dalit. 'It was you who was tasked with the girl's disposal . . .'

'I know nothing of the ruby, my lord.' Dalit's reply slid out as slippery and smooth as custard. 'The basket containing the child was handed to me by her nursemaid, after we brought her to this country. I left the basket outside the workhouse, as you commanded.

'I do not know how it got there, but someone must have hidden the ruby in its box. Sadly it is not possible to question the nursemaid, since she was disposed of in the Thames shortly afterwards, as you may remember.'

The fat man grunted, and Dalit changed the subject. 'Was it not a risk to bring the girl here? To let her see the animals?' he asked.

'Ha! Ha!' The chins bobbed and bulged in time with the

fat man's high, tinkling laughter. 'It amuses me to show the princess what a fine profit we have made from the beasts of her kingdom! The kingdom she will never see! There is no risk – look at her; like a dumb animal, she remembers nothing!'

But he was wrong about that. The part of Fly that had spent its life fighting to survive – even though it was buried deep – was fighting the poppy syrup. And as the carriage set off for home, a crossing-sweeper stuck fast to its highly polished bottom, everything she had seen and heard was stored away in the back of her head.

CHAPTER 9

'Stop drinking the tea!' The tiger's teeth bared in a snarl; his patience was running thin. Being back behind bars was taking its toll.

It was the morning after her visit to the menagerie, and Fly was drifting past his cage with the same vacant expression she'd worn for days. The tiger had started to despair of waking her from her poppy-trance. The only good thing was that the golem seemed to have stopped shadowing her so closely. Clearly the fat man had decided Fly no longer needed such careful watching now he believed she and her ruby and her tiger were all under his control.

At least she looked at him this time. But her black eyes were dull, with none of the dancing mischief they'd had when she'd dropped out of the chimney and into his cage.

'Come closer,' the tiger commanded, having got her attention.

Fly looked around her. After so many days of breathing in the evil in this house, she'd taken on the habit of fear along with the habit of silence.

'Don't be frightened, it is not watching you,' the tiger growled impatiently.

Something flashed in Fly's eyes. 'I ain't afeard of nothing!' she said, automatically.

'There she is! My princess!' the tiger whispered. 'Come closer, then,' he repeated.

She shifted towards the bars on slipper-muffled feet.

'Closer,' the tiger insisted.

At last she was close enough. Like lightning, the tiger lashed out through the bars and drew his claws across her heart. Surgically precise: enough to shock her out of her poppy-dreams, but not enough to kill.

Fly looked down at the deep rips in her tunic. Blood bubbled up, staining the yellow silk scarlet. It seemed like it was the first real thing she had seen for days.

There was a moment's silence, then . . . 'I told you it weren't blue!' she said. And grinned. It was like picking up a conversation where they'd left off, days before. The tiger grinned back.

'You have to stop drinking the tea!' he said again.

She nodded.

'And then we have to leave.'

She nodded again. 'The animals,' she said, slowly, as the memories of the last few days trickled back. 'They're being sold . . .'

'When?'

'In four – no – three days, now . . .'

'Then we must leave soon.'

The focus returned to her pupils as she looked round. For the first time since she'd been brought here, she checked out the exits. 'This place has got more locks than Newgate,' she observed. She grinned again. 'Don't suppose you've twigged where they keep the keys?'

'I don't think it will be that simple, this time,' the tiger said. 'These locks are controlled by more than simple keys. You will have to use your powers.'

Fly's face clouded. 'I can't do the stares no more, not when he's around.'

'You must practise,' urged the tiger. 'You must make your powers stronger than his.'

Fly's fingers brushed against something soft in her pocket. It was the feather. How had it ended up there, with the daily change of clothes, even when Fly herself had forgotten it? She remembered the gasp the servant girl had given when she saw it, and she wondered . . . had the girl put it there? Had she too been trying to make Fly remember?

The fog was lifting from her brain with every throb of pain from her chest. 'The ruby,' she remembered.

'Ruby?' A shadow passed over the tiger's face.

'That's what were inside my box – my box from the workhouse, what Black Bill kept hidden. A bang-up slumdinger of a ruby!' Fly explained. 'It fell out of the chimbley, when I was hiding and the fat man . . . the fat man, he says it's his now . . .' She shuddered, but then gave herself a shake. 'But it ain't his, it's mine! And the box only opens for me, any road!'

The shadow deepened in his face, but the tiger made no comment.

She paused, then, eyes shining, she went on, 'When I touched it, it were like touching you, like it could frizzle off my dib-dabs! Like I could do anything!'

The tiger growled and the stripes on his face darkened into a frown. 'Do not let it fool you! Learn to rely on your own powers!'

But Fly wasn't listening. 'I reckon that ruby could beat anything he's got up his havey-shavey silk sleeves. I reckon the ruby can get us out of here!'

The tiger sighed. 'You must be wary of that thing. If you insist on taking it with us, you must use it wisely . . .' Then his round ears twitched as if he had heard something. 'The golem is approaching,' he said. 'Go quickly. Hide your scars.'

Fly had stripped off her yellow tunic and was trying to stem the bleeding when she heard, too late, soft footsteps behind her in the bathroom. She spun round.

'Blimey, don't no one knock around here?'

The girl was staring, horrified, at the cuts on Fly's chest. Then she looked at Fly's face, and when she saw the real Fly glaring back at her, she looked even more scared.

Fly pulled out the feather. 'It was you what put this safe, in my kecks, weren't it?'

The girl nodded.

'Blister it, I wish I knew your name!'

The girl took Fly's hand. Watching Fly's face, she began tracing letters on her palm. For someone with as small an acquaintance with the alphabet as Fly, it was a struggle, but eventually she made out the letters.

'Z-A-L-I-Y-A. Zaliya?'

The girl nodded. She mimed as if her wrists were fastened together, and then broken apart.

Fly frowned. 'Break . . .?'

The girl shook her head, frustrated. She made a quick running movement with her fingers.

'Free . . .?'

The girl nodded and pointed at herself, and the palm on which she'd written her name.

'I get it! That's what your name means – Zaliya – it means "free"?'

Zaliya nodded. Fly's eyes blurred like they had in the menagerie, and she turned back to the sink and splashed water on her face. Then she faced the girl again.

'Listen, Zaliya, I don't rightly know what your story is, and it don't look like you'll ever be able to tell me, but I don't reckon as you likes this shummocky set-up, no more than I do.'

The girl shook her head.

Fly paused. How far could she trust this girl? But she really could do with some help getting out of this place. She made her decision. 'Look, I is planning to scarper – skedaddle – do a flit – you know.' She could see the doubt on Zaliya's face. 'Don't rightly know how yet,' she admitted. 'But I is trusting you not to go snitching to His Nibs.'

Fly tried a cautious grin. And the girl smiled back, trying it on like a hat she'd left behind a very long time ago, in another place. She picked up Fly's torn and bloody tunic and went out. When Zaliya came back, she was still trying out the smile, and she was carrying bandages and another set of clothes. Dark red this time.

'Smart thinking, girl!' Fly wriggled them on, wincing. 'Won't show the blood.'

Surprisingly, Zaliya winked.

CHAPTER 10

The fat man's house stood, disguised by its ordinariness, in a row of other mansions on the edge of London. But where the stonework on the other houses had been painted a fresh white and the doors a cheerful red, the fat man's house was a forbidding black, and the heavy front door was painted to match. There was nothing welcoming about this place.

As Fly began to shake off her poppy-haze inside the house, anyone observing the outside of the house that day might have noticed an unusual amount of activity in the street. There was an uncommon concentration of street urchins hanging about with apparently very little to do.

The crossing in front of the black metal railings had never been so well-swept. There were never fewer than two crossing-sweepers hard at work, though they were very careful to keep out of range when the fat man stepped out of the front door, brandishing that metal-tipped stick. 'Out of my way! Filthy little mud-pushers!' And they were quick to skedaddle when his carriage tore off without pausing to check if a child might be crushed under the wheels.

The mudlarks, Tree and Cess, had set themselves up in a new line of business, and were busy selling bunches of violets on the corner. But they didn't ask the fat man to buy. 'He don't look like a man who's very fond of flowers!' Tree observed.

'Don't nobody ask that cove for no tips,' Spud had warned them all. 'Or you'll end up brown bread like little Jimmy, pushing up the daisies.'

By the evening, when there were no passers-by in the street to observe them, the front wall of the house was crawling with tumblers, who were hanging upside down from the gutters like a colony of bats and peering in through chinks in the shutters. Sparrow's house-breaking skills came in handy when it came to shimmying up drainpipes and finding ways to open windows that people didn't want opened.

The wall opposite was propped up, as if he thought it was in danger of falling down without his support, by a long, thin figure with one knee bent behind him. Stick did not appear to be doing anything very useful at all, but while he chewed on the empty pipe in his mouth, his brain was whirring away at the best plan to get in and out and rescue Fly. He had no idea what that mirksy cove wanted with the closest thing he had to a sister, but he wasn't going to let a few locked doors stand in their way.

Fly, drawing up her own plans inside, knew nothing of all this. Until, late that night, as she wrapped a fresh bandage about her chest, she heard a cautious knock at her window. She drew the heavy curtains to see Sparrow's face pressed, upside down, against the glass. The grey wool cap that she'd last seen on Spud's head was now stuck firmly on his, defying gravity.

She gaped at him, as he grew increasingly scarlet and bulging about the eyes.

'Boil me, Fly! Let me in or me head will explode!'

Fly slid the sash window open and Sparrow swung himself inside, quickly followed by Spud, who had been holding on to his ankles from the roof. Stick came swiftly after. She was about to close the window, when Sparrow leaned out and gave a whistle, and more gutterlings came tumbling in – Tree and Cess, Squinty and Bandy. In the end there were seven of them standing there, wriggling their bare toes in the thick carpet and staring round like they'd landed in the bedroom of King Billy.

'What the blazes, Stick – you brought the whole town with you, or what?'

'Thought you might be in need of company in this naffy new crib of yours, Fly!' said Stick.

'You going to treat us to a spot of supper, Fly?' added Sparrow, always on the lookout for the possibility of food.

Fly put her finger to her lips and pointed to the four-poster bed. Nobody said a word until they'd all climbed in, and the thick curtains were drawn around them to muffle their voices. She got out a barrel of sugar-coated biscuits that was refilled by Zaliya every morning. Everyone took a fistful and handed it on, but it somehow got stuck when it came to Spud.

Then they all sat gawping at Fly, like they were down The Cut on a rainy midnight, waiting for another ripsmasher of a story about her latest narrow escape. Except this time she hadn't got away.

'Lawksamussey, Fly, ain't you the dandy? Look at your swish togs an' all!' Cess and Tree stroked the satin sheets and patted Fly's pale pink nightgown. 'Don't rightly think her needs rescuing!'

'She looks like a blancmange,' said Stick, with less enthusiasm, echoing Fly's own thoughts on the subject. 'And what's happened to your hair?'

Fly scowled and tousled her black hair, to make it stand up like it usually did when it was sticky with soot. But it just sank back flat against her head, as soft and smooth as everything else in this silken prison.

'They keeps making me wash,' she said, in apology. Her nose was twitching. She'd never noticed the ripe smell the gutterlings carried about with them before.

'Where's that tiger?' asked Sparrow, nervously.

'In a cage downstairs,' said Fly. Sparrow looked relieved, but Fly knew it was her fault the tiger was back behind bars. Her hand pressed the raw slashes on her chest, and she winced.

'What's that fat man want with you, Fly?' asked Stick, quickly. He'd seen the wince. 'Word on the street is that he's a right dicey cove.'

'I dunno.' Something that Fly would never have admitted was fear passed over her face. How to explain it all, when she didn't understand any of it herself? All that baloney about magical powers and blue blood and a lost kingdom, and the ruby. All they saw was the same little street tyke, no different from usual, except she was clean. But for her, everything had changed.

Tree and Cess had lost interest and crept out from the curtains of the four-poster to explore the bathroom next door, with muffled squeals of delight over all the sweet-smelling soaps and brightly coloured bottles. The rest of them were looking increasingly uneasy.

'We needs to get going, Stick.' Sparrow had given up trying to get the biscuit barrel away from Spud; he tiptoed back to the window. 'Quick in and out, that's what you said. The watch comes past here every hour, I been on the lookout.'

Bandy and Squinty went to get the girls, who were filling their pockets with stuff to sell on the street. They all lined up waiting for Fly and Stick at the window.

'Come on!' Sparrow already had his leg cocked over the windowsill. 'If we hustle, we'll be back down The Cut by midnight.'

'Mebbe Fly can liberate a bit of fried fish for us, for our supper . . .' Spud joined him at the window.

Stick was still sitting next to Fly on the bed. 'Where's your kecks, girl?' He was watching her face. 'Ditch the blancmange togs, and slip out the windy with us, easy as treacle.'

It would have been that easy. A hop over the windowsill, a helping hand up to the gutter, and a slide down the drainpipe to freedom. Back to the old life, back to using the stares to thieve a living on the streets. But Fly had changed. She had a tiger pacing through her heart.

'Look, it ain't as simple as that, Stick,' said Fly, quickly. 'The fat man – he's got my . . . you know, that box we went to get from Black Bill's . . .'

She knew the gutterlings would understand about her wanting to hang on to portable property, since none of them had ever owned anything in their lives. Although she also knew that if she told them there was a ruby inside the box, Spud would be all for flogging it so they could treat themselves to a slap-up dinner.

She added, slowly, 'But it ain't just that . . .' She paused. 'I can't leave my . . . I can't leave the tiger.'

She was certain sure none of them would understand about the tiger, but Stick just looked at her, saying nothing. She remembered then how he'd looked at the tiger, back in the old warehouse, and how he'd been the one who went up to Smithfield to steal bow-wow mutton, to make sure the tiger got fed.

Outside they heard the watch approaching. 'Eleven of the clock, and all's well!'

Stick nodded. 'We'll wait 'til he's past,' he said, quietly. 'Bring your leg in, Sparrow – it's not considered a normal thing, round these parts, to have a leg hanging out the windy.'

Sparrow pulled his leg in, but Fly knew that he and Spud were twitching to be gone. Time was money, and they'd missed another night of tumbling to rescue her. As for her, she was like Sparrow's leg, half-in, half-out, desperate to leave but knowing she had to stay. And knowing she needed their help.

'Look, Stick, it's not just the tiger. There's all these other animals, what the fat man's got locked up, and he's selling them to these toffs, I have to save all them too . . .'

Fly stopped to breathe, flummoxed for a moment by the difficulties that faced her. 'I needs you to find me a ship.'

'A ship?' Stick got to his feet, staring at her.

'Yeah, a ship. To take all the animals home.'

'Is you loose in the attic, Fly? What doolally juice has he been feeding you on? You need mint sauce to pay for a ship. And we don't none of us have a tosser to our name, 'specially when we ain't been tumbling for days . . .'

'It's all rug, Stick, I can get the dibs, if you find the ship. But the animals is being moved in three days – I needs that ship real quick!'

Stick's grey eyes looked at her, and for that long moment Fly held her breath. Then he nodded, and she knew that if it could be done, Stick would do it.

After Fly had watched the gutterlings disappear one by one out of the window, she climbed back into her pink blancmange bed. The slippery silk sheets clung stickily to her skin, and she longed to be back in the rickety old warehouse, tucked up warm with her tiger. He seemed a very long way from her, locked up in the cage down below. And the notion of getting a ship and sailing away with all the animals seemed like an impossibility.

But then Fly remembered how much she loved an impossibility. She was still grinning as she fell asleep.

CHAPTER 11

Fly eyed the aspidistra anxiously and poured another cup of golden tea into its pot. She had to be ready to leave in two days.

'I hopes you don't mind the poppy juice, mister,' she apologised to the plant in a whisper. 'But I reckon it's doing you a power more good than it were doing me.' Indeed the leaves of the aspidistra were looking a lot less droopy. As was Fly, without it.

The servants who were bringing in her breakfast took no notice. She might have been imagining it, but since she'd told Zaliya she was planning to escape, they seemed friendlier, casting odd, shy glances and smiles at her whenever the fat man wasn't around.

Fly needed to get her stares back, but trying to use them in this house was like swimming through treacle, such was the power of the fat man's magic. This morning, to her great relief, he had gone out early to arrange for the transport of the animals. It was easier to practise when he was gone.

She wandered out to the hall. But her first attempts at concealing the tiger from the servants – mere child's play to her a few weeks before, when the pair of them had slid unnoticed through the city's alleyways – didn't go so well.

'Drabbit it,' Fly muttered as she tried to control her straying, slippery thoughts. 'It's like prigging eels out of a barrel. No sooner has I got the stares by the tail, they wriggles away and there's nowt left but the heads.'

One minute she thought she'd got it and the tiger was nothing but a large shaggy mongrel, the next minute the stares slithered out of her control and the tiger was back. For a good half-hour Fly's stares got stuck, and the bewildered servants scurried through the hall not daring to look at the strange half-dog, half-tiger that was gazing at them from between the bars of the golden cage.

Fly slumped against the wall, exhausted with the effort of trying to push the poppy-sweetness out of her head.

'You do not have time to rest.'

By now there was nothing left of the tiger but a disembodied mouth, floating in mid-air. *But it don't seem to shut him up from nagging me,* Fly thought, crossly. *Mebbe I should just make him disappear.*

'This is not a comfortable feeling,' complained the tiger's mouth. 'You are making me look ridiculous.'

Fly looked at him and sniggered. 'You don't exactly look like a king of beasts, now,' she admitted, but then she was sorry because the mouth stalked to the back of the cage and refused to return. 'Go away and practise on something else,' the mouth snarled.

The trouble was, she knew he was right. She didn't have time to rest. In two days, the animals would be gone.

I needs to get all of them eels back in the barrel, and keep them there, she thought, frowning. *Start with something smaller, girl,* she told herself.

She wandered into the dining room where the servants were clearing up after breakfast. Soon she had plates of kedgeree and kippers appearing and disappearing before the very eyes of the dumbflustered servants. *They thinks the whole house is betwaddled.* She grinned in satisfaction as she made her way upstairs to her room to practise some more.

Zaliya was less easily fooled, when the pile of bright silk tunics she was putting away in a drawer turned into a tray of piping hot muffins. By now she had learned to expect the unexpected from Fly. Fly sat on the bed, spluttering with suppressed laughter. Zaliya gave her a stern frown.

Fly grinned. 'Sorry.' The muffins turned obediently back into tunics.

But even after practising all day, as soon as the fat man was back in the house, she felt the dread of the golem return and her strength fade. In the evening, after a silent dinner, the fat man made her sit with him in the airless drawing room while the stuffed animals whispered to her. 'You didn't save us . . . you have to save the others . . . only two days left and they will be gone . . .'

The fat man waved his hand at the wall and took out her box from the safe. 'Show me!' he demanded, and she could not help but obey him. He watched with those greedy little eyes, like dimples in greasy dumplings, as the box fell open at her touch and the dark room was lit with the glow of the *Nga Ran* ruby.

In the ruby's glow, Fly forgot everything. She thrilled to its sweet seduction, hardly noticing when the fat man sank down next to her. They gazed into the ruby's heart together, side-by-side, both bewitched by the beauty of the thing. She forgot the tiger's warning, she forgot how much she hated the man whose rolls of flesh were pressed against hers. The ruby warmed her like the poppy syrup, sucking her into its heart.

'You is so beautiful,' she whispered to it. She forgot the

animals, due to be sold the day after tomorrow. She forgot the servants and their lost tongues. She forgot even her tiger, pacing in its cage, aching to be free. In that moment, the ruby possessed her.

But then the fat man took it from her, and the flame dimmed and went out the moment it left her hands. Fly got up. She felt suddenly sick, as though she had eaten a barrelful of toffee apples.

'What deep magic is this?' the fat man muttered, as he locked the ruby away. And somewhere, deep inside, a bit of Fly sniggered in delight at his frustration, because the ruby worked for her and not for him.

The tiger's golden eyes were blazing as she passed through the hall to go upstairs. His pupils were narrowed to pin-pricks and he gave a low growl, deep in his chest.

'I told you to be careful of that thing.'

She looked away. For the first time since she'd fallen into his cage at the menagerie, Fly, who was afraid of nothing, couldn't face her tiger.

She was shaking when she got to her room, and in her dreams that night, the tiger was walking away with never a backward glance. And no matter how fast she ran, she could never catch up with him.

When she crept downstairs next morning, the tiger was lying in the dark at the back of his cage with his eyes closed. There was something desolate about the slump of his shoulders, and his golden stripes were entirely swallowed up by the black.

'I swear I'll get you out of there,' she whispered, but the tiger barely stirred.

A rap came at the front door, and Dalit glided into the hall to answer it. Fly squared her thin shoulders. *Keep grinning like a gigglemug, girl*, she reminded herself as she fixed on the doolally look she'd become practised at wearing. But she didn't feel like grinning. She'd had no word from Stick about the ship, and time was running out for the animals. They would be moved tomorrow.

A messenger was at the door with a letter bearing an elaborate golden seal. Dalit placed it on a silver plate and carried it through to his master in the drawing room, glancing at Fly as he passed.

He left the door slightly ajar, and Fly dawdled over and hung about to listen outside. The tiger was still ignoring her, but she saw his round ears twitch, and she knew he was eavesdropping as hard as she was.

'A letter from Prince Harmoud, my lord,' she heard Dalit announce.

'From the king, you mean,' the fat man corrected him sharply.

Fly heard the sound of a paper knife slicing open the seal.

'Indeed, my lord, the king.' Why did it sound like Dalit was sneering?

A pause, then, 'Excellent! We are to return home at last, Dalit! His Highness is well pleased with the fortune we have made for him over the years, from the sale of so many animals. But he is eager now to see the ruby.'

'Does he not fear the curse, my lord?'

A slight intake of breath, then a tinkle of laughter like fingernails scraping down a slate. 'That is nothing but superstitious nonsense! There is no curse! Now, go and start packing.'

But Dalit wouldn't shut up. In fact, his voice was getting louder. 'And the girl? Does she return with us?'

'Don't be a fool, Dalit. She is all that stands between the king and his throne, once her father is gone. And he cannot last much longer. Once the king has seen the ruby and knows it is truly the *Nga Ran*, why bother to keep him alive?'

'But how will you open the box and get the ruby, if the girl is dead?'

There was a swish of a heavy cane, a suppressed cry of pain.

'Enough questions, slave! I should have cut your tongue out with the rest! The girl will open the box for me tomorrow, before the sale of the animals. And then you can take her and throw her in the river. Who will miss one more guttersnipe, floating in the Thames?'

Outside in the hall, the tiger lifted his great head and looked at Fly.

'Time to go then, my princess?' He grinned and Fly's heart skipped like a herring escaping back into the sea. The fat man might be about to snabble her, but her tiger was talking to her again.

She nodded and grinned back. 'I reckon we'd best mizzle tonight! Or I'll be brown bread by the morning!'

CHAPTER 12

'You'll know it's him – he's the one with the knees what don't meet in the middle.'

Fly's patience – not something she'd ever had much of – was running out. And the girl with no tongue was getting in more of a pucker and a fluster, the more impatient Fly became.

'Drabbit it,' she muttered. 'What a slow-top!' But she needed Zaliya's help.

'His name's Bandy, and he's right outside,' she explained again. 'You just have to slip out the back door and go round to the street-crossing – that's where he's waiting. Then you give him this!'

Fly and Stick had agreed that she could get a message to him through the crossing-sweepers, who were still outside the house, on what was by now the cleanest crossing in London. But she hadn't reckoned on how long it would take to persuade Zaliya to take the message.

The words had been strung together, with great concentration, from the few letters Fly had picked up between beatings at the workhouse.

BEIN KILLT TERMORRER. GET SHIP REDDY. MEET MIDNITE.

She just hoped those other professors of learning, Stick and Spud and Sparrow, would have enough combined bits of letters to make the message out. And that they'd remember the meeting place. Because there was no way she had enough letters to spell 'MENAGERIE'. And no way they'd be able to read it.

She watched from her window as Zaliya, looking as guilty as if she was off to kill the king, finally got the courage to creep out and stuff the bit of paper into Bandy's hand, before scurrying back to the house. Bandy looked up to Fly's window and waved to show that he'd got it, and then set off at a lick to find the tumblers.

Now all she could do was wait for nightfall. And let herself wonder what the fat man had meant when he'd said 'He cannot last much longer . . .' All that stuff she had overheard at the menagerie began to come back to her. Could it be that somewhere, she had a father, and he was still alive? *Fiddlesticks and gammon!* she told herself, fiercely. She had no father. Nor no mother. She weren't going to fall for any of that bunkum.

'Dalit – I dine out this evening with Lord Turnwit, to discuss the final details of the sale tomorrow,' the fat man announced over the dainty tea he insisted on, sharp at four, every afternoon. 'So very English, so very civilised!' he exclaimed, as he did every day while guzzling down cakes, in that same high, sweet voice that a few hours before had ordered Fly's death.

Fly had to stuff a couple of éclairs into her mouth together to cover her grin when she heard the fat man would be gone all evening. She had to admit they were good éclairs. *Going to miss all this prog,* she thought. *Ain't never ate this well.*

Dalit bowed. His eyes kept straying towards Fly. She hoped he hadn't noticed what she'd been doing with the golden tea a moment before, pouring it behind a cushion at the back of the sofa.

It was almost nine before Fly dared to creep down the staircase into the darkening hall. The house was finally quiet, but there was only an hour to go before the fat man and Dalit were due back. She'd shuffled off her silks and left them coiled around her slippers like a coral snakeskin, before putting on her old rags, which she'd kept hidden under the bed. *Cor, they'll smell me coming in this clobber!* she thought, as her nose adjusted. But then she remembered that everyone else she knew smelled just as bad. She brushed the scarlet feather soft against her cheek, before tucking it safely into her pocket. *Hang on! I'm coming for you. I promise.*

The tiger had been dozing, but now he slowly lifted his head to look at her. The anger was gone, but for the first time she noticed the woefuls in his dimmed eyes. All these days back behind bars had taken their toll.

'Time to get gone!' she whispered, and he rose, his stripes rippling bright in the shadows as he shifted towards the door of the cage.

'Open it,' he rumbled. She could tell that he shared the excitement that was bubbling up in her chest. As long as she could overcome the fat man's magic on that lock, he would be free, and she would feel him pacing beside her again, his strength flowing through her once more.

But then Fly heard it. Before the tiger could even warn her, it was there: a whisper of pure evil. It was the golem. The fat man must have left it behind to guard her. Dalit had been watching her like a hawk – had he told the fat man that she was up to something?

Fly's skin crawled, and she looked into the tiger's eyes in panic. 'It's here!'

'You have to look at it,' insisted the tiger.

'I can't, I can't,' whispered Fly.

'You are afraid.' The tiger's whiskers twitched.

'I ain't!' swore Fly, suddenly furious. 'I ain't! I ain't afeard of nothing!'

And she made herself look.

There it was at last, worse than anything she had conjured in her nightmares. A hideous thing of horror slithering towards her, faceless and shapeless as smoke, framed against the brightness of the tiger's coat. It was a soulless thing, a thing that might once have been human, but which now was a slave to evil.

Fly's knees turned to junket and she clutched at the bars of the cage to stop herself falling. She couldn't breathe. If she took a breath, she would breathe it into her and it would be inside her for ever.

'Don't let it in!' growled the tiger. 'Have courage!'

'I'm trying!' she gasped. She clutched for the tiger through the bars. His warm strong flank pressed against her hand, and she felt the sparks fly up into her heart once more.

'You must use your powers to open the cage. Once I am free, I can help you.'

Using her powers to unlock the cage was even harder than putting on the stares. It was like seeing through stone, and she was still trying to stop the golem from seeping into her soul.

'Fight it!' roared the tiger. The roar was as every bit as rib-rattling as that first roar back in the menagerie, and Fly felt in that moment that it was her roar too. And the lock sprang open.

With a bound, the tiger sprang at the golem, and it scuttled away into the shadows and was gone.

'We must go quickly,' the tiger said. 'Before it comes back with its master.'

Fly was shaking and faint, and all she wanted was to get out of that terrible place, but there was something she couldn't bear to leave behind. 'The ruby!' she gasped.

The tiger snarled and she backed away, but there was a stubbornness in her eyes as she faced him.

'I wants my ruby,' she said defiantly, trying to keep the tremble out of her voice.

The tiger paused. Then he sighed. 'Very well. If you must.' That shadow was on his bright face again.

Together they slipped into the drawing room. Fly waved her hand at the wall. Nothing happened. 'How the mischief does he do it?' She waved again. Still nothing. 'I looks a right jobberknoll, waving at a wall!' she wailed. 'It ain't no good! The wall don't listen to me!'

'*You* are not listening to the wall!' insisted the tiger. 'Use your fingers and feel for the edges, if you want the ruby that much.' There was something like disgust in his voice.

Fly put her hands up to the wall and tried to block out the terror that the fat man might return at any moment. She felt a faint buzz, like the ruby was calling her. *It's like the stares, girl,* she said to herself. *Put the stares on the wall.*

Minutes ticked by, as she fought down the panic. Every sound outside in the street made her jump and shattered her concentration, and she had to breathe deep and start over again. But at last the solid wall melted away beneath her fingers, and the opening appeared.

She reached in and took out the box. It fell open when it felt her touch; the flame leaped up in the heart of the jewel and filled her with bravado. She felt like she could take anyone on, holding this. It was hers.

She turned to show it off to the tiger. 'Look! Ain't my ruby a beauty!' she boasted.

The tiger gave it a glance and looked away, curling his lip in that way Fly had forgotten. 'It is a just a stone. It is only people who value such things. And that is what turns them into a curse.'

'Gammon!' Fly muttered under her breath, but she snapped the box shut around the ruby and tucked it into her waistband. She turned her back on the tiger and started heaping gold from the safe into one of the soft bags inside.

'No!' the tiger growled, deep in his throat.

'What do you mean, no?' Fly ignored him. She was still in a huff, and she kept stuffing in the gold, remembering all those hungry, cold nights on the streets.

'No!' This time the roar filled the room, and Fly was thrown back against the wall with the force of it. 'That gold does not belong to you!'

Fly pushed herself to her feet, gaping at him. 'But the fat man made all this gold from selling the animals! Animals like you!' Her voice was shaking. The glass eyes of the stuffed, dead animals glinted in the candlelight. But they were not saying whose side they were on in this argument.

'It is stealing. No good will come of it. A princess does not steal.'

'That baloney!' the old Fly was about to say, but then she hesitated. The old Fly was still there, all right, but all that gammon about her being a princess was making her wonder. *But I don't have time to think about that right now,* she thought. *And any road, even princesses need mint sauce.*

'We has to have the dibs to pay for the ship!' she protested. 'How do you think we is going to get you all home, with nowt but air in our pockets to pay the captain?'

'The ruby. We give him the ruby.'

Fly stared into the tiger's unwinking eyes. Not her ruby! How could he expect her to give up her ruby? It was the only thing she had ever owned. It felt like he was asking her to rip out her heart.

Long moments passed and his golden eyes never left hers. It was like he could see right inside her. She thought about the sweet power of the ruby coursing through her veins. But then she remembered how the ruby had made her feel like she'd eaten too many toffee apples, and she sighed. She didn't understand, and she knew that Stick and the rest of them wouldn't understand either, but she knew she had to trust the tiger. So she put the bags of gold back and closed the opening, without another word. There was a loud purr from her companion as they left the room.

'Hurry!' said the tiger.

But she didn't need hurrying. The golem would have warned the fat man by now, and the carriage would be tearing back through the streets towards them.

Fly turned her stares on the front door, and the bolts that had been bewitched by the fat man's evil slid silently open, and the locks tumbled. But then, just as they were about to step out into the freedom of the sweet night air, Fly felt a touch on her arm.

Fly never screamed, because she was never scared. But in that moment, when she thought they were caught and their bid for freedom was over, she very nearly screamed. She took a deep breath and turned.

It was Zaliya.

Fly swore. 'Blimey, girl, you fair frighted me into convulsions!'

But then she saw the rest of them. All the silent servants, in a row, staring at her, their eyes as full of woefuls as the tiger's had been.

Zaliya pointed at Fly's heart, and then her own, and then she swept her arm towards the others before pressing her hands together in a silent prayer and bowing her head to Fly. The rest of them did the same. Then they all kneeled down.

'What in tarnation do we do now?' Fly asked the tiger. The servants were behaving like she was their queen or something.

'They are your people, your majesty,' the tiger said. 'They know you are their princess. You have to take them home with you.'

How long had the tiger known that his home was her kingdom? Was it since that first lick, when he had tasted her blood? Fly's head was full of questions, but then somehow it didn't seem to matter. Because she knew, with a heart-leap of joy, that she and the tiger were going to face this adventure together.

CHAPTER 13

'Blister it, how the blazes are we going to rescue the animals with this lot in tow? It's like herding sheep!' Fly had never herded a sheep in her life, but the only difference as far as she could tell was that this lot weren't bleating.

'Wotcher, Fly!' Bandy and Squinty popped up, grinning, from behind the bushes. 'You brought a few friends?'

'Blest if I knows what to do with them!' Fly said helplessly. The servants stood around her in the street, gazing at her in silent trust. 'We needs to get going!'

The crossing-sweepers grinned. 'That's all rug, Fly – Stick said for us to hang about, in case you needed a hand. We'll take them down to the docks – Tree and Cess have been sorting out a ship. Tumblers are waiting for you up at the menager-roo.'

Fly turned to the servants. 'Go with Bandy and Squinty,

they'll look after you,' she said. They still stood staring, doubtful. 'Cor, love-a-duck!' muttered Fly in frustration. 'Go! Now! We will meet you at the ship!' She wasn't sure where that voice came from, but it worked, because they all turned obediently to follow the sweepers. 'Blimey, I is turning into a right termagant!' muttered Fly, but when she turned back to the tiger, he was purring again.

'Climb on!' he said, and this time Fly didn't hesitate. She sank her fingers into his thick coat and wrapped her skinny legs tight around his back, as strong as armour. It was like coming home.

The wild gallop through the dark streets blew the last of the poppy syrup and the fat man's heavy magic from her head. Her black eyes danced as she clung to the tiger's thick neck, and the joy of freedom surged like lightning through his shoulders and into her heart.

Putting on the stares was child's play for Fly out here on the streets. She giggled at a couple of crushers who gaped like a pair of nick-ninnies at what they thought they'd seen, before she persuaded them that the tiger was nothing but a pedlar's moke cantering home for a late supper.

The familiar figures of Sparrow and Spud were practising cartwheels in the quiet street when Fly and the tiger galloped up to the doors of the menagerie.

'Do not let go of me!' warned the tiger, as she slipped off his broad back. 'We must not let the golem find us.'

'Bust me, Fly! Where you been?' Stick pushed himself off from the wall he had been propping up opposite the menagerie, stuffing his empty pipe away in what was left of a pocket. 'It's getting late – Captain says we have to leave by four to catch the tide!'

'You found a ship, then?' Fly twisted her fingers tight in the tiger's coat.

'Course we found a ship! Said we would, didn't we?' Stick made it sound as if it came as natural as dipping pockets. 'It's the same captain what brought the animals here – reckoned a cove like that would know what to feed them all on, and he's got all the cages and all!'

Fly saw the tiger's lip curl. 'He is an evil man!' he rumbled. 'And we will not need cages!'

Stick only heard the growl, but he didn't like the captain any more than the tiger. 'He's a right dicey cove, Fly – it's all about the mint sauce with him. I reckon he'd sell his granny for a turnip. Have you got the dibs?'

'Course I have – keep your hair on!' She showed him the box, tucked safely into her waistband. 'I reckon what's in there'll be enough to keep him sweet.'

Stick nodded grimly. 'Let's hope so.'

There was a hush in the darkness of the menagerie as they stepped inside. It felt like the silence of despair. It had been many weeks now since these beasts had seen the sun or felt the wind. And many months since they had been stolen from their homes.

Fly had made quick work of the locked door. The tumblers were used to Fly lifting vittles for everyone's supper without stall-keepers seeing a thing, but even *they* stared as she made the door-lock tumble with a single glance.

'Blimey, Fly, we could all set up in business as house-breakers, after this!' whispered Sparrow.

The tiger just curled his lip.

The guard, as usual, was half-seas over, snoring like a grampus afloat on an ocean of empty bottles. 'Tie him to his chair, Spud,' said Stick. 'He'll not put up much of a fight.'

Rustles and soft whimpers started up around the dark cages; the animals had come to fear the sound of human voices.

'What now, Fly?' The tumblers were all looking at her.

'Let them all go, I suppose,' she said, although she had no more idea than them, never having freed a menagerie of wild beasts before. 'And just hopes they follows us!' She handed out the keys.

It took a rallying roar from the tiger to bring the animals out. When their cages first swung open, most cowered away at the back, fearing the fat man and his stick. But slowly, slowly they prowled, trotted, shambled and swung themselves out into the centre of the menagerie, and stood gazing at Fly and the tiger.

'Phew!' Stick whistled as the assorted beasts assembled in front of them: elephants, lions, giraffes, zebras, monkeys and a couple of camels with humps as droopy as their faces. 'You haven't half gone and done it this time, Fly! This'll be a one slumdinger of a story to tell of an evening, down The Cut!'

Fly had to agree, but then she thought that she didn't rightly know whether she'd ever be telling tales down The Cut again. And she wasn't sure how she felt about that.

At last only the birds, chattering excitedly over their heads, remained to be freed.

'Come on, Fly, we needs to mizzle!' The tumblers were itching to get gone. 'Leave them! We got the animals!'

The guard had been woken by a pair of golden monkeys, who were getting their revenge by pulling what was left of his greasy hair and tweaking his red, bulbous nose. A third one was pouring the last of the gin over his head.

He started to his feet, shouting like a madman, but he was still tied to the chair and he ended up on his back, kicking his legs. He had the air of an overturned tortoise.

'He'll get you for this!' he spluttered. ''You don't want to cross His Lordship!'

'Come on, Fly,' urged Stick. 'He's going to bring the crushers down on us!'

Fly looked up, touching the scarlet feather in her pocket. There was stuff in her eyes that was stopping her seeing straight. 'I can't leave them! They're breaking their hearts up there!'

She grabbed a heavy shovel. 'Open them big doors and get ready to go. I is going up to get the birds.'

The tiger followed her up the stairs, as he had once before, and they climbed the metal steps to the roof together.

'Watch out, my cullies!' she called down to the birds, as she took the shovel and smashed it down on to the soot-stained glass roof.

Shards of glass splintered and showered into the net below, and a brilliant rainbow of birds rose up into the sky. Up and up they flew, towards the dawn-dimming stars, and Fly thought for a moment they would just seize their freedom and be gone, and she would never see them no more. But then they gathered in a many-coloured cloud and swooped back over Fly's head. There they hovered, waiting for her word.

'Let's go!'

Back in the street, Fly climbed on to the tiger and they led the way through the rapidly lightening streets towards the docks. They could not gallop this time, in spite of the need for haste. Putting the stares over this lot was like throwing a blanket over the sun, and Fly needed all her concentration to cod the early-morning workers on the streets into seeing nothing but a bunch of country boys herding their cattle to Smithfield, and a milkmaid riding on a donkey.

'How's she doing it?' The tumblers followed, gaping like guppies, but after a few streets with no one taking any note beyond a good-morning, Spud, who now had the cap back, started tipping it gaily at passers-by in greeting. 'Wotcher!'

The docks were a foreign country for Fly and the tumblers. It was a place where the ships seemed to have got ashore and the houses seemed to have got afloat and all were jumbled together in a bewildering forest of rigging and masts.

The little cavalcade with its accompanying overhead flock, disguised as drab London sparrows, stumbled to a halt at the entrance to the docks. Fly didn't know where to go, and with every moment that passed, the sky was brightening towards the dawn high tide. If they missed this tide, they would be stuck. The fat man would find them and all would be lost.

'Where's the ship, Stick?' Fly was frowning with concentration. 'Me head's busting!' In the past she hadn't had to hide much more than a muffin, and never for this long.

Stick looked as confused as she did. 'I dunno, Fly. It's called the *Dark Destiny* or something, but I can't see it.'

Then there came a cry. 'Over here, Stick!'

It was Tree. 'Cripes! Thought as you were never going to make it! Captain's in a fair old tweak over something – says it's 'cos we'll be too late for the tide, but Cess reckons there's something else. She says high tide's not for two hours, and she knows this river like the back of her hand. He's a real havey-shavey cove – I don't trust him, Stick.'

'He'll be all hunky-dory once we show him the mint sauce, Tree.' But Stick didn't look like he trusted the captain any more than she did. 'Fly's got his money . . .'

Tree led the way, weaving nimbly between the jutting figure-heads whose carved faces leered down on them out of the early mist from the river. This was her territory. Everywhere she went she was greeted by seamen and dock-workers, and she skipped and dodged over the reels of rope wound round the heavy bollards that had the rest of them tripping up every few steps.

'Courage, girl!' whispered the tiger, under his breath, as Fly slumped for a moment on his shoulders, exhausted with the effort of protecting the animals.

The servants were gathered by the *Dark Destiny*, still looking very much like a flock of sheep, with Bandy and Squinty as their shepherds. Only Zaliya managed a small smile. The rest just looked miserable and nervous, still not really believing they could ever escape the master who had taken their tongues and stolen their lives.

'Croopus, he's got a face like a hatchet!' muttered Fly, when she saw the captain waiting for them on the dock. He had a hook for a hand and a hook for a nose. His dark skin, under something that had once been a tricorn hat, had been beaten to old leather by sea-spray and tropical suns. He wore what might in more respectable days have been a uniform, but was now exceedingly worn and disreputable about the seams.

'All he needs is a parrot and a wooden leg, and he could be a pirate,' Fly remarked to Stick.

'Not much difference, any road, I reckon. He's shavey enough to be a pirate,' replied Stick. 'Just show him the money, Fly.'

Fly slipped down from the tiger and was about to pull out the box, when the tiger growled, 'Do not give it to him until the animals are on board. This man is planning to double-cross you. I smell it on him.'

'Where is the money?' called the captain, impatiently. 'The tide'll be on the turn!' Tree was right; this man could hardly stand still. He was hopping about like a barrel of weasels, he was so anxious to be off.

Fly stepped towards him, forgetting to keep her hold on the tiger. She was no longer bothering to disguise the cargo. The captain knew all about the animals anyway.

'It's in here!' She showed the captain the box, but she didn't open it.

'It's just an old box,' sneered the captain, making as if to snatch it, but a snarl from the tiger behind her was enough to make him jump back.

'You can see the dibs when we is all stowed ship-shape on board.' Fly was doing her best to speak sailor.

The captain scowled and hesitated, the dark creases gathering into a thunder-cloud in his face. Fly held her breath. Why should he believe that a sweepling like her could possess such a fortune? But he couldn't take his eyes off the box. Fly reckoned that the ruby was playing along, and was calling to him, and greed and doubt twisted in his clenched jaws.

'Get the cargo aboard, Barkus!' he grunted to the ship's mate, who was standing waiting for orders.

The tiger padded over to encourage the animals, but they needed no persuading. The ship's crew watched in amazement as the beasts they had beaten and whipped into cages on the voyage out made their way gaily up the gangway, the monkeys taking a ride on the elephants and clinging to the tall necks of the giraffes. The silent group of servants followed, and the birds flew up and roosted on the rigging, making the ship look as though it was festooned with bright ribbons.

'Ready to cast off, Captain!' called the ship's mate from the deck, above their heads.

The tiger padded half-way up the gangplank. 'Come, girl!' His tail twitched with impatience.

Fly turned to Stick. He and the rest of them – sweepers, mudlarks and tumblers – had lined up on the dock like a row of soldiers waiting to take the royal salute.

'Come on!' Fly's black eyes were sparkling. 'Let's get on board.'

Stick shook his head. 'We ain't coming, Fly.' It was his turn to possess the grey wool cap, and he was twisting it in his hands, not looking at her.

'Don't be daffy!' Fly's stomach caved in and it felt like the dock had turned to water under her feet. 'I can't go without you!'

The idea of undertaking this adventure alone had never entered her head. Any new kingdom would be no kingdom at all, without the tumblers. Who would she tell her tales to, of an evening?

'Where you is going, it's not for the likes of us.' Stick took a breath and looked her straight in the eye. 'You're different, Fly, you has always been different. The rest of us, we is just gutterlings, and these is our gutters. This is our home . . .'

Fly never cried. In a fury, she scrubbed at the stuff that was trickling down her cheeks. The tumblers were the closest she had ever known to family. Stick was the brother she had never had.

But then a sweet, high voice behind her blew all other thoughts out of her head.

'You have my ship, I think.'

It was the fat man. Dalit stood behind him, grim-faced, glancing up at the rest of the servants on the deck.

'Drabbit it!' Fly had let go of the tiger for too long. He let out a great roar from the ship's deck, but she knew he was too far away to help her. She took a breath and forced herself to look round. The golem was slithering towards her, ready to take possession at last. She didn't know whether it was better or worse now she could see it. *You ain't having me*, she thought, grimly.

'Captain!' the fat man called out to the weevily, moth-eaten old seasalt, who was backing away towards the gangplank. 'There has been some mistake. The *Dark Destiny* was promised to me.'

Fly twigged now why the captain had been in such a hurry to be off.

'You seem to have my property – and also my servants – on board,' the fat man continued smoothly. 'Have your men put those animals in their cages, at once, and see to the unloading! I have a customer waiting.

'And have those – those . . .' He almost called them people, then decided they didn't deserve it. 'Have my slaves put in chains.'

The captain stuck his thumbs in his belt and slanted his narrow eyes at the fat man. 'Well, sir, 'tis like this. It be my ship. And if an individual do come and show me the colour of their money, and it be a considerable amount more than what you is accustomed to pay, then I as captain do have to take into account what be right for myself and my crew.'

Fly saw out of the corner of her eye that the ship's crew were swinging themselves down by ropes to stand behind him. They looked every bit as villainous a bunch of varmints as their captain, but it looked like whatever he decided, they were ready to back him up.

'Now,' the captain went on. 'Let's have both of you show me what you're prepared to pay, and we'll be off with the tide.'

The fat man laughed with that absurd tinkling little laugh that set Fly's teeth on edge. 'Dalit, the gold.' Dalit returned to the carriage and came back carrying the bags of gold Fly had left in the safe.

The fat man poured the gold coins into a shimmering heap on the dockside. 'There, fellow, will that satisfy your greed?' He turned and smirked at Fly.

He knows I have the ruby, she thought. *But he don't in a week of Wednesdays believe I'd give it up.* Slowly she pulled out the box from her waistband.

The sky was pink with dawn now, but the glow of the early sun was eclipsed by the red glow of the *Nga Ran* ruby as the halves of the box fell open. A gasp went up around the dock, and the captain took a step backwards.

'Don't be a fool! You cannot give that away!' spat the fat man at Fly. 'You have no idea of the value of that ruby – how many men have died to possess it! Your father lost his kingdom for it!'

Fly had never seen this snake so rattled before, and she would have laughed, but the golem was slithering closer. She gasped, focusing all her strength on holding it at bay.

Fly looked down at the flickering heart of the ruby. Her next words were the hardest she'd ever spoken. 'The ruby is yours,' she said steadily to the captain, 'If you gets us all safely home . . .' 'Home' was a word she'd never used before, and it tasted strange on her tongue.

The golem fell back, as if it had lost some power over her.

The captain was transfixed by the ruby. 'Beats your gold into a cocked hat, mister.' He strode towards the gangplank. 'Best get on board sharpish, girl. The tide's running and we're ready to cast off.'

The fat man was creeping closer to Fly on those tiny feet, as dainty as devil's hooves. Dalit was close behind him, his dark shadow.

'Watch out, Fly!' called Stick, taking a step towards her.

'It's all rug, Stick. I ain't afeard of him.' She was, but she knew there was nothing anyone else could do for her now. She had to find the courage to fight the fat man alone.

He made a guttural command, and sent the golem slithering back towards Fly. She backed away, towards the gangplank and her tiger, never taking her eyes off the golem for a moment, barely breathing lest she breathe him in.

'Come, child,' urged the tiger from the gangplank. He gathered himself to spring. His snarl stopped the golem, but the fat man was still coming. His powers overwhelmed Fly and she froze, just as she had back there in the chimney when he first took her prisoner.

Before the tiger could leap, the fat man lunged at her, but at that same moment Dalit sprang at his master, pinning him to the ground. Together they rolled towards the edge of the dock, Dalit grunting with the effort of holding the fat man down.

Fly watched, transfixed. She still could not move. The servants were all hanging over the side, watching Dalit struggling for his life.

He's one of them! Fly saw it for the first time. *Dalit hates his master as much as the rest of them.* She remembered suddenly all those questions Dalit had been asking the fat man. He must have *meant* her to hear. He had been on her side all along, and she had wasted her time hating him as much as she hated his master.

'Help her!' the tiger roared, and the grey wrinkled trunk of the largest elephant snaked down from the ship and wrapped itself around Fly's waist, lifting her bodily to the deck. The tiger sprang up after her, and the crew swiftly pulled up the gangplank.

Below, the struggle between Dalit and the fat man continued. It was a fight to the death. Dalit lifted his head, as the fat man's fingers closed on his throat.

'You are the true princess,' he gasped, his eyes staring up at Fly, glassy in death. 'Find your father and take back the throne. End this wickedness.'

With a final groan, he rolled himself and his master off the dock, and they plunged together down into the river. As the *Dark Destiny* pulled away, the bodies of the fat man and Dalit were sucked into the swirling waters under the keel and disappeared. The golem was nowhere to be seen.

Fly could hardly bear to look back at Stick and the rest of them, watching from the dock. Something was breaking inside her.

'Come with me!' she called, desperate. 'We'll have such larks, Stick!'

But the gap between ship and land was too wide now. Stick shook his head and waved, and Fly scrubbed her wet cheeks and waved. The words she wanted to say were lost on the breeze that was blowing out towards the sea.

PART TWO

CHAPTER 14

'Why the long face, girl? What you blubbing about, snotty-nose?'

Fly scowled and squinted at the bag-of-bones boy with skin as dark as her own, who'd dropped to the deck beside her like he'd fallen out of the sun.

'I ain't blubbing! I don't never blub!'

The boy grinned and that made Fly scowl deeper, 'cos he put her in mind of Stick, and she didn't want to think about Stick.

'Why you so wet round the winkers, then, child?' The boy squatted comfortably on his haunches. He didn't seem bothered by the rough swell which had kept Fly heaving into a bucket since they set sail two days before. He looked like he was settling himself down for a proper chinwag, and she scowled again to put the frighteners on him. It didn't seem to have much effect.

Fly was in a rare old humdudgeon, and she wasn't ready to part company with it yet. Here she was, sailing to some blame-fool land she knew nothing about, on a ship that she hadn't dared look over the side of since they'd left the hug of the Thames, and which had no exits that didn't end up in the ocean.

She had nothing left of her ruby but the empty box. The ruby itself was locked away in the captain's cabin, and she knew she'd never clap eyes on it again; she blamed the tiger, who'd not been near her since she'd snapped at him their first day on the ship and called him a flea-bitten old rug.

'If you are going to be a princess, you would do well to start behaving like one,' he'd growled as he stalked away, and what was so aggravating was that she knew he had a point. All she really wanted was to wrap her arms around his strong neck and feel his rough tongue drying her face, which seemed to be permanently wet these past few days, and not just with sea-spray.

'You ain't stopped snivelling since you came on board, child!'

Fly glared at the boy, but he wasn't going away. She went on the attack. 'Who you calling a child? I reckon you ain't much older than me, even if you can fly up and down them nets like you was born with feathers and a beak.'

She narrowed her eyes against the sun to get a better look at him. He was much the same height as her, with wiry limbs and spiky black hair. The difference was that her hair was longer now. She ruffled hers in envy but she couldn't make it stick up like his any more.

She didn't want to admit it, but she'd been watching this boy dancing through the rigging with envy. *Cor, he beats them tight-rope walkers up the circus!* she'd thought. As soon as they got on board, the golden monkeys had scampered to join him up there, leaping from mast to mast, chattering with delight and chasing the birds until they soared away into the sky, only to return and settle out of the monkey's reach. They all looked so happy to be free, and the truth was, she wished she was up there with them, instead of down here with nothing but her blue devils for company.

The boy threw back his head and laughed. 'They ain't nets! We call them "ringeen", or "rigging", chil—' and she could see he was about to call her a child again, until he saw the fury in her face and thought better of it. 'What do they call you?'

'Fly,' she muttered.

'I'm Jack!' He pointed to himself, to make sure she understood, like she was touched in the upper works or something. 'Do you want some chow?' He made as if he was putting food in his mouth and pointed below deck.

'If you means "prog", I ain't hungry,' Fly replied, still on her high horse, but then she realised that she was actually ravenous.

'You'll feel better by and by!' Jack pointed at Fly's bucket. 'I was sicker than a shotten herring, first time on board – I thought I was half-dead'

Fly grinned at last. 'I felt like I was all dead!' Despite herself, Jack was making her laugh. 'I bin lobbing me groats into that bucket since I got on board!'

'You'll need some chow – some prog – then.' Jack grinned back and held out a hand to pull her up.

She scrambled to her feet. For the first time, she didn't feel sick. 'Where's the kitchen?'

'We calls it the "caboose"! Or the "galley"!' Jack corrected her.

'What's the matter with King Billy's English?' muttered Fly, but she let Jack lead her below decks to meet the cook, who looked like a wizened little walnut, bent almost in half, so he was no bigger than Fly. He was flinging pans around in a space that would barely have passed for a cupboard on land.

Never seen a skinny cook afore, thought Fly, as he dolloped a ladleful of something that put her in mind of workhouse gruel into a bowl. *Mebbe he don't fancy his own cooking.*

'What the devil is it?' The grey stuff was so thick her spoon was standing up in it.

'It be good chow, missy! Best lobscouse!' The little walnut gave Fly a curious stare, and then turned back to his bubbling pans – all of them full of lobscouse.

Fly was none the wiser, but clearly there was nothing but lobscouse on offer, so she followed Jack back up to the deck with her bowl and squatted down next to him, her back against the ship's side. She liked it better that way; she couldn't see the sea.

'It's nibblish good!' she declared, after the first lumpy spoonful.

'You hungry or what?!' Jack watched, gaping like a guppy, as Fly shoved down spoonful after spoonful, without taking breath. But Fly's mouth was too full to respond.

At last she wiped her lips and sighed. 'Blimey, me guts thought me gizzard had been cut!' She scraped her spoon round the bowl and licked it clean. 'What's in it?'

Jack shrugged. 'Plenty of lob. Not much scouse!'

Fly laughed again. It felt good to laugh.

All around her, she could hear sailors cursing and calling to each other in rich mix of languages. 'But they all talk

Pidgin as well,' Jack told her, when she looked puzzled. 'Everyone can understand Pidgin, don't matter where they come from.'

'How long you been a sailor?'

'Since I was little,' Jack replied. 'I was just found, outside this orphan-place. Soon as I could walk, they sent me to sea.'

'Me too.' Fly nodded. 'Where was the orphan-place? Where you from?' *Mebbe he's from the same place as the tiger,* she thought. And then a very quiet voice in her head added, *And the same place as me.*

But it was the wrong question. 'Nowhere. I ain't from anywhere.' The wide grin, that had reminded her of Stick, faded in an instant.

'Jack! You lazy chuckeroo! Get your skinny backside aloft afore I skin it for you!' It was the first mate, who seemed to be next down in command from the captain, because he was the one giving all the orders on deck. He pointed up at the rigging, but the rest of what he said about fore-masts and mizzen-masts and top-gallants and staysails might as well have been Pidgin for all that it meant to Fly. Jack sprang to his bare feet and leaped up the rigging and was gone, before she could ask him any more questions.

With a wistful look upwards, where Jack was flying once more between ropes and rigging, Fly picked up the bowls and took them back down to the caboose. The gnarled old cook lifted his head from the steaming pans and nodded at her, with the same curious look he'd given her before. 'Thankee, missy.' Nobody had ever called Fly 'missy' before. It had always been Fly – or something a lot worse.

Now that she wasn't heaving her guts into a bucket, Fly realised that everyone on board was giving her the same curious looks. The sailors stared at her, nodding their heads as she weaved her way unsteadily along the deck. Fly had spent her life trying to avoid being seen, because mostly whatever she was up to had been against some law or other. She wasn't enjoying all this attention, and she ducked her head down and kept her eyes on the deck, which had the added advantage that she didn't have to look at the sea.

She found the tiger at the other end of the deck, sprawled lazily on his side, watching some zebras, who were watching him very carefully back. The only bit of the tiger that was moving was the very tip of his tail, which twitched now and then; every time it twitched, the zebras twitched too.

'You're teasing them.' Fly was reminded of the horses on the number 10 omnibus. 'They thinks you going to eat them.'

The tiger looked hurt. 'They know I won't eat them!' he protested. 'I gave my word!' Then he looked back at their fat rumps, like they were a row of shiny humbugs in a sweet shop. His pink tongue curled out, and his mouth yawned red, and his sharp white teeth glinted in the sunlight – and the zebras scattered to the other side of the deck. 'Not while we're on the ship, anyway.'

There did seem to be some kind of truce between animals that would normally have seen each other as fair game for dinner. A couple of lions were lying nearby, as lazily as the tiger, watching the zebras and the giraffes with unblinking eyes. They were basking in the sun, which had grown hotter the closer the ship sailed towards the equator. They lifted their nostrils to the warm breeze; if lions could smile, this lot were definitely smiling.

'They are all happy to have their freedom,' said the tiger. 'Apart from them . . .' He nodded at the pair of camels with drooping humps.

'What's wrong with them? They've got mugs like dying ducks in a thunderstorm!'

'They've got the hump,' replied the tiger, and then gave something that sounded like a little snort. He gave Fly a sly look under his long lashes.

She stared at him. 'Was that a joke?' She could have sworn the tiger was hiding a smile under his long white whiskers.

There was a silence between them. The tiger seemed to be waiting for something.

'I come to say sorry.' Fly scrubbed awkwardly at her black hair. 'I were being a brat. And you ain't flea-bitten.' She paused and said softly, 'You is the most beautiful thing I ever saw in my whole life.' Fly had found out very early on back in the menagerie that the tiger liked a bit of flattery and flummery, but this time she wasn't saying it just to stay alive.

The tiger stood up and stretched himself slowly, first front legs, then back. He reared up and rested his great paws on her shoulders, making her stagger for a moment with his weight. His golden eyes gazed into hers for what seemed like an age, then . . . 'Your face is dirty,' he said, and he licked away the tracks of her tears.

After that, the pair of them stood together looking out over the endless waves, for what seemed like an age. Fly felt safer with the tiger's warm body pressing against her skinny legs, like it had once before, when they'd looked out towards the sea from the old warehouse. She knew he was thinking, as he had then, of the home that lay beyond all that ocean, but she had no idea what lay ahead for her, once he found his freedom.

The emptiness of the ocean scared the stuffing out of her, she who had happily thieved her way through the most villainous backstreets and most murderous alleys of London. She had a sudden vision – her first since she had stopped taking the poppy syrup – of a wall of green water, high as a house, rearing up like a dragon to swallow the ship, and the animals and the servants screaming to her for help as they plunged, terrified, into the sea. And she couldn't help them, because she was sinking, down and down, seeing the last of the golden sun floating above her head as her lungs filled with water in place of air.

Fly had never got on well with water. She shivered and twisted her fingers through the tiger's deep fur. 'Blimey, who'd have thought there was so much of the perishing stuff! Is the animals not scared?'

The tiger shook his heavy head. 'Anything is better than those cages,' he said. 'Whatever happens, at least we'll all die free.'

That sort of freedom didn't much appeal to Fly. 'Clobber me if I is going to snuff it down there with all them creepy fish!' she muttered. 'I is not going to end up as supper for some haddock!' She had always hated those gaping open mouths and blind staring eyes on the fishmongers' slabs down Billingsgate Market, although she had to admit she was partial to a bit of fried fish when she could nick some for her tea. She only had the vaguest idea of what lived under the sea, but she hadn't forgotten the corcodile what had swallowed that sweepling in the Serpentine.

'I ain't a-going to think about it!' She turned her back firmly on the waves and looked around for something to do. Back on the streets, there wouldn't be an hour that went by without her and Stick fettling up some sort of wheeze, and Fly was bored.

It was feeding-time for the animals, but the captain had faced a mini-mutiny on the first day, when the crew had refused to go anywhere near the wild beasts that would normally have been safely behind bars.

'Get them quiet coves to feed them,' the captain had snarled at the mate, before shutting himself up in his cabin to gaze at the ruby. 'They can't complain – and who'd miss them if they gets eaten?'

So the silent servants had been put to work, and so far nobody had got eaten. In fact, Fly thought, as she watched them handing out the food, they looked as happy as the animals. They had all escaped the clutches of the fat man, and they were all going home.

But then the ship lurched alarmingly and listed to one side, as the elephants led a small stampede for the bales of hay.

'You addlepated bunch of sapskulls!' the first mate shouted down from what Fly later found out was called the quarterdeck. 'Them jumbos can't all be starboard at the same time!'

'Keep your hair on!' Fly shouted back. Taking a guess at what he meant by starboard, she seized a fork and started distributing the hay more evenly around the deck. 'Here, jumbo, over here!' The largest of the three elephants, the one that had snatched her up to the ship, followed her, and she rubbed its trunk to say thank you, before turning to show the servants what to do. 'Look, spread it round like this, before the jumbos land us in the drink!'

But then the fork was gently but firmly taken from her hand. She turned, laughing, thinking it was the younger elephant playing a game. 'Here, I were just using that . . .'

But it wasn't the small elephant. It was her former maidservant, Zaliya, and all the other servants were standing behind her. She pointed at the fork and then at Fly and shook her head. All the others shook their heads in the same way.

'Drabbit it!' Fly turned to the tiger. 'Why is they all in such a pucker and a fluster?'

'They don't think it is right for their princess to work.' The tiger watched Fly's face.

Fly considered what she knew about royalty. She thought about old King Billy, bowling along in his golden coach with his face buried in a hankersniff to keep out the smell of his people. And she thought about all the gutterlings hunkering down in doorways tonight without Fly to prig them a hot pie. And she thought about all the hot pies that the ruby could have bought them.

'Does a princess have to do as she's told?' she asked the tiger.

'No,' said the tiger. 'She has to do what she thinks is right.'

So Fly shook her head right back at Zaliya and the rest of them, took back the fork, and carried on feeding the animals.

CHAPTER 15

Fly might have won the right to help feed the animals, but at bedtime Zaliya insisted, in her own silent way, that since Fly was their princess, she should sleep like a toff, in a tiny private cabin next to the captain's.

Not wanting to hurt Zaliya's feelings, Fly had obediently headed into the cabin that evening – then she'd crept back to the tiger after the warm tropical dusk turned to night. She didn't know what was going to happen when they arrived where they were going, and she wasn't going to waste her remaining time with him. She tucked herself up snug against the tiger's warm belly, and fell asleep to the rhythm of purring, deep in his chest. But she made sure Zaliya found her back in bed in her cabin at dawn.

In fact, Zaliya still insisted on behaving like she was

Fly's maid, and the tiger had said she'd better get used to it, if she was going to be a princess.

'Blest if I know what to do with a maid!' Fly had retorted.

'Some decent clothes wouldn't go amiss.'

The tiger's black lip curled in disapproval and, taking a good look down at herself as they lay there under the stars, Fly could see his point. Half of her bare bottom was hanging out of the rags that Black Bill had begrudged her. *Mebbe that's why the crew keep staring at me like I've got two heads,* she thought.

'Can you make me some of them britches, like Jack's got?' she asked Zaliya, the next day.

Zaliya sniffed and the disapproving curl of her lip put Fly in mind of the tiger, but sure enough, there was a pair of thick navy cotton britches – with the scarlet feather tucked carefully in a pocket – waiting for her in the cabin by morning, together with a loose white shirt, just like Jack's. Fly had completed the transformation by stealing Zaliya's scissors and hacking her hair short, so it stuck out in tufts every which way.

Ain't I the dandy in me new togs! Fly was thinking as she stepped out of the cabin, ruffling her cropped mane.

'Git aloft, lad! What you doing idling down there on the tootuk when you should be aloft sorting out the ringeen!'

The first mate's voice boomed down at Fly from the quarterdeck.

Was he talking to her?

'Is you deaf or daft, lad? Get aloft!' His face was red with fury.

He thinks I is Jack! Always game for a wheeze, Fly leaped up and swung herself along the rigging.

But once she was there, things were a lot more complicated than Jack had made them look. After she'd mixed up her mizzen-mast with her mainmast and her jiggers with her jibs, Barkus was almost apoplectic with rage. 'I'll blister you when I ketch you!' he yelled. 'What you playing at, you little toe-rag?'

'You're turning everything top-side down!' Jack came swinging easily down to rescue her and chucked her the right rope.

'I has made a bit of a mux of it!' Fly admitted, catching hold.

'You're making too much bobbery!' agreed Jack. 'Hold your gab for once, and watch!'

With Jack's teaching, after a couple of hours Fly started to get the hang of things, and whichever of the Jacks the first mate threw an order to, the job got done. They made a good team. Each of them seemed to know without words what the other one was going to do next.

'You hungry?' shouted Jack, as the sun scorched down at midday.

'Could do with some chow!' Fly agreed – she was getting the hang of sailor talk – and they slid down the rigging and landed together at the feet of the first mate.

'Blister me – there's two Jacks!' Barkus swore, gaping at Fly and Jack standing next to one another. He'd not realised he'd been shouting orders at two of them. 'You're as alike as a pair of knaves in a pack of cards!'

Fly looked at Jack and Jack looked at Fly. *He's got a face like a heart*, thought Fly, but then neither of them had ever looked in a mirror, and they were hungry, so they just shrugged and went down to the caboose for a bowl of cobbily-mash. Which seemed to Fly to taste much the same as lobscouse.

After they'd eaten, Fly went to help feed the animals, so it wasn't until almost sundown – which came sudden and early near the equator – that she scrambled back up the rigging to find Jack.

He was sitting in the crow's nest, keeping lookout with a spy-glass. The sea was almost flat calm, and you could hardly tell where sea ended and sky started, apart from the red glow where the sun was sinking into the west. The little golden monkeys were lolling about lazily in the rigging, the setting sun crimsoning their coats while they picked contentedly at each other's fleas. As Fly climbed, her bare feet curling confidently around the rigging now, one of the giraffes reached up and nibbled gently at her toes with its soft lips.

Overhead the birds were circling, reluctant to leave the sky and settle for the night, but when they saw Fly they dipped down and brushed her face with their wings as they swooped past.

'They is saying thank you.' Jack was watching them. 'They loves you.'

Fly's face felt hot and she looked away. 'Why do all them sailors keep staring at me?'

'The ruby,' Jack said simply, as if that was enough.

'What d'you mean, the ruby?' she prompted him.

'Everyone in Barithea knows about that ruby,' Jack went on.

'Barithea?'

'The country you is going to, clod-pate . . . the place we is sailing to . . .'

'Barithea . . .' Fly tasted the name on her tongue. 'What's it like?'

Jack shook his head. 'I never goes there.' It didn't seem like he wanted to talk about it. He went on, 'The ruby's bad luck. It's cursed.'

'It's not been bad luck for me,' argued Fly.

'You gave it away.'

Fly wasn't sure if that was a question or an answer, but she nodded, with a pang of loss.

Jack went on, 'The captain, he likes that ruby very much. Too much. Won't leave his cabin.'

'Is that why the first mate's come over so curmudgeonly? Because he's had to take charge of the ship?'

Jack nodded. 'And the crew is going off their chumps, too. They all thinks about nothing but the ruby, all day. And how much mint sauce they'd have if they took it off the captain! That ruby makes trouble.'

'That's what the tiger said,' Fly said, without thinking.

Jack looked up at her quickly. 'You can talk to the tiger?'

It wasn't just surprise in his face. It was a kind of hunger. *But not for lobscouse*, she thought.

'Kind of . . .' she answered, cautiously. She'd never told anyone about talking to the tiger. She didn't want Jack to think she was loose in the attic. It mattered to her, somehow, what Jack thought. It mattered a lot.

She gave him an uncertain grin. But Jack turned away and went back to scanning the dimming horizon. It was the same as when she'd asked him where he came from – he'd shut himself up like a clam, as if he'd revealed more of himself than was safe.

'What the devil?' Jack quickly pushed the spy-glass into his shirt and slipped out of the crow's nest.

'Sails ahoy!' he shouted to the crew as he scrambled down the rigging, pointing out to sea. 'Black sails on the horizon!'

The presence of those black sails, day after day, never coming closer but never letting them out of its sight, darkened the mood on the *Dark Destiny*. Or perhaps the mood had been dark ever since the ruby was brought on board, and Fly had only noticed since Jack's warning.

'Do she draw closer?' The first mate had his own spy-glass constantly to his eye, but he also had Jack running up and down to the crow's nest every hour, to check what the ship with the black sails was doing.

Still it came no closer, nor ever let them out of its sight.

'Cap'n? Cap'n?' Barkus had to hammer on the captain's cabin door before he was finally let in. But he came out afterwards muttering curses and shaking his head. 'He thinks of nowt but that blasted ruby!'

'The captain's just sitting at his desk with the ruby in front of him, gabbling at it like a loon,' Fly reported back to the tiger, after peering in through the cabin window. 'I reckon as it's betwaddled his brain!'

'It does that to people,' the tiger agreed.

The crew stood about in groups, and no matter how many floggings Barkus handed out, less and less work seemed to get done on board. The general opinion that Fly heard muttered was that the ship with the black sails was a pirate ship that had got wind of the ruby. They all thought the pirates were just waiting for the moment to strike, before they reached port. 'But I reckon as this lot are dicey enough to steal the ruby off the old skinflint themselves, and beat any pirate to it!' Fly told the tiger.

Still, day after day, the ship with black sails came no closer, nor ever let them out of its sight.

'Ships' sails is meant to be white,' she whispered to the tiger. 'What sort of mirksy varmint puts up black sails?' If Fly hadn't seen the fat man being sucked to his death in the Thames, the dread she was feeling at the sight of those sails would have convinced her that it was him who was coming after them.

The tiger didn't comment. She went on. 'It can't be him. He's dead. He's dead, ain't he?' She wanted the tiger to tell her not to be so daffy, that it couldn't be the fat man, but he still didn't say anything. His great weight pressed against her legs, but it wasn't the same comfort as usual, especially when he just shrugged and turned away.

'You must be ready to fight for your kingdom,' was all he said. But he didn't say whether he would be there to fight with her, or how she was going to do it.

The first mate gave the order for the *Dark Destiny* to hug the coast so as to be able to make a dash for the nearest port, if the ship with black sails made a move. As they drew closer to the shore, the breeze brought Fly her first scent of a different sort of earth – spiced and sweet and strange. With the smell of land so close, the mood amongst the animals shifted between hope and almost frantic impatience to get off the ship. At night, with nothing but the waves around them, they had been silent, but now the darkness was punctuated by the howls and chatters of animals giving voice to an unbearable homesickness. And calls came back from the land, maddening them all with longing.

'How many days 'til we reach home?' Fly asked Jack, on a rare moment she managed to catch him alone. With the mood of mutiny in the air, Jack was the only crew member the first mate trusted by now, and Barkus kept him busy. But Jack also seemed to be avoiding her, like he was scared of something.

'Home?' He scowled and snapped at her. 'Why do you call that place home?'

'I dunno.' Fly looked away, because she didn't want him to see what was in her eyes. She remembered one of the first things he'd said: 'I belong nowhere.' Then she insisted gruffly, 'It's what the tiger calls it, so I does too.'

But Jack's words had reminded her that she'd made no plans about what she was going to do, once the animals were safe. What was she to do? *Find your father*, Dalit had said before he fell to his death. But how would she do that alone? The tiger would surely want to leave her the moment his feet touched the earth of his homeland.

She desperately wanted to tell Jack about her blue blood and the half-heard truths about being a princess and having an uncle who wanted her dead – and maybe even a father who was still alive. But he was already on his way back up the rigging.

'Two more sunsets. Then we'll be at the place you calls home,' he called down to her. 'It is a very bad place. With a very bad king. He sells his people for slaves and his animals for gold.' He scrambled higher and shouted down, 'I never goes there. And if you got the sense you was born with, you won't neither.'

CHAPTER 16

The first dark shadow fell on the deck as Fly was practising her stares.

'You have been neglecting your skills,' the tiger had warned her earlier that day. 'You will need them again soon.' She had been lying in the sun with her head on his warm flank, soaking up the contentment that oozed from him ever since he had got back his freedom. Whenever she wasn't up the rigging with Jack, she'd spent every moment she could with the tiger.

But there would soon come a time when she'd look back and wish she'd had more.

There had been something in the tiger's voice she couldn't argue with. She knew in her bones that something was about to happen. The tension on the *Dark Destiny* had been humming in the heat like a hornet's nest. By tomorrow at dawn they would be in port, and she could already see the rocky shores of the land that the tiger called home. Barithea. The land that was supposed to be her kingdom.

So she'd been distracting herself, while keeping a wary eye on the crew, by practising the stares. She was hiding bales of hay from the servants. 'Now you sees it . . . now you don't!' The elephants weren't fooled for a moment – they knew exactly where their hay was – but it fooled the servants, who were struggling to deliver the morning feed that had somehow become betwaddled and bewitched.

Fly felt a drop of rain land on her head and squinted up, past Jack, who was high in the rigging, silhouetted against the sky. Storm clouds had been gathering since dawn, darker than any they had seen during the weeks they had spent at sea. But the cloud that blocked out the sun had now taken on a shape that made her skin prickle; the shadow it cast looked like the head of a dragon. There was a rumble of thunder and the still air cracked with electricity, like the sparks from the tiger's coat.

'God's fish!' she swore. 'What's that?' At first she thought it was the sound of heavy raindrops on the deck, but then there came confused shouts, running feet and a rattle of musket-fire. As the rain started to lash down, she made out the first mate, standing squarely with his back to the door of the captain's cabin. He was shouting defiance at a grimly determined band of sailors. Two of them were pointing muskets at his chest.

'Stand aside, Barkus, our business bain't with you!'

'It's the cap'n we wants to see – and that ruby he swore to share with us!'

'We be almost in port – it's time to settle up!'

But the captain's door remained firmly shut. It looked like he was leaving the first mate to face this mutiny alone.

Fly could smell the rising fear amongst the animals. They were restless under the onslaught of the rain, and the crack of gunfire and the rolls of thunder were greeted by terrified squeals from the zebras and snorts of fear from the giraffes. The elephants shifted nervously from one great foot to another, their harrumphs of anxiety punctuated by low growls from the lions, but up in the rigging, the chattering of the golden monkeys had fallen silent. The camels pursed their thick lips and maintained their gloomy silence, like they had never expected this to end in anything other than disaster. The eyes of every animal were on these men, waiting for what they would do next.

At Fly's side, intent but silent, the tiger was fixed on the stand-off between the crew, his black pupils narrowed as he watched every movement. For one long moment he took his gaze from the men and looked up at Fly with those golden eyes, and it was as if she could see right into his mighty heart. She was to remember that look, in the long lonely days that lay ahead.

Fly stepped forwards to block the gangway between the crew and the animals. She pushed her tiger behind her, resisting the urge to sink her fingers deep into that thick coat and cling to him. He could protect her from many things, but not men's guns. Behind her, she saw all the freed servants following her lead, standing square in front of the animals they had looked after for weeks now.

Fly took a deep breath to find the strength, and threw a blanket of stares over her animals and her people. 'They just wants the ruby,' she called back, to reassure them all. And herself. She wanted the sailors to forget they were there. This wasn't their quarrel. 'They just want the ruby, they don't want us!'

It was growing darker, as storm clouds hid the sun, and rain like ramrods lashed the ship. Huge waves reared up over the sides and flooded the decks. Fly braced herself and held fast to the side of the ship. She wasn't going to move from her post, but it was getting harder to keep up the stares with every moment, and in truth, she could do nothing to protect her animals and her people from the storm.

There was a tearing sound from above – the wind was ripping the sails, in fury at anything that stood in its path.

'Jack!' Fly cried. She could see his thin frame braced against the mast as the ship rolled and bucked with every towering wave. The little golden monkeys were clinging to him, chattering now in terror. *The birds!* thought Fly. *How can the birds survive this?* They were wheeling helpless against the wind, bright tatters of feather and bone being tossed ever closer towards the mounting waves.

The storm was adding to the confusion amongst the mutineers, who tried again to shift the first mate away from the cabin door. 'Don't be a blame fool, Barkus – get out of our way . . .'

Barkus turned and hammered on the captain's cabin door. 'Cap'n! Cap'n! You has to show them the ruby, or we'll all be dead on the rocks!'

Fly suddenly understood his fear – while he was fighting off this mutiny, no one was steering them through this storm. So close to land, the ship would be wrecked for certain.

At last the cabin door was flung open. In a flash of lightning, Fly glimpsed the captain's haggard face. He looked like a man possessed, his eyes glinting red in the reflection of the ruby he was clutching to his chest.

The sight of the ruby was like lighting the fuse to a heap of gunpowder. There was another rattle of musket-fire and Barkus dropped like a stone. The men swarmed over the body to seize the captain, and in the commotion he lost his hold on the ruby and it rolled away across the deck. He fell to his knees like a beggar and all the sailors fell to their knees and scrabbled after him.

But Fly cared nothing about that, because a great green wall of water was rearing up in front of the ship like the chest of a dragon – but bigger than any dragon she had ever invented, in even the tallest of her tales. She looked up and screamed 'Jack!' as the dragon's head struck the mainmast and the last thing she saw was Jack falling, falling, still hugging the smallest of the golden monkeys to his heart as he plunged down into the sea.

Ahead of her, the ship tilted until it was almost standing upright, trying to climb up the wall of water. At last Fly could hold on no longer, and was sent sprawling backwards towards the tiger. Somewhere she felt his strong body behind her, and heard his great roar, as she reached out to try to wrap her arms about his neck. In a flash of lightning she had a last glimpse of Zaliya and the others clinging to the terrified animals. Their shrieks were whipped away, lost in the howling of the wind. And then came the crash of splintering wood on rocks, and the towering chest of the dragon collapsed down on the ship, and they were all gone, washed into the boiling, writhing waves.

It was very still and dark and silent under the waves. Fly watched, fascinated; a string of bubbles like precious pearls trickled up from her mouth as she plunged down. She kicked her legs, like she had back in the Thames on that moonlit night, when the tiger taught her to swim, but nobody was playing now, and she couldn't feel the tiger beneath her this time. Her head broke above the surface and she called out to him, 'Tiger! Tiger!' But another wave crashed down on her and her lungs filled with water in place of air, and she sank down and down. And the sun broke though the storm clouds and floated on the sea, a long way above Fly's head.

In the distance, the ship with the black sails came no closer but waited in the safety of the open sea. And somebody watching on board put down his spy-glass with a smile of satisfaction, as the *Dark Destiny* sank to the bottom, taking with it every soul on board.

CHAPTER 17

Fly vomited until she thought her guts were going to join her on the beach. 'Blimey, I'll be inside out in a minute . . .'

She hiccupped and swallowed hard to try to keep her stomach where it rightly belonged. But still she kept her eyes shut tight, because she wasn't convinced that she hadn't woken up dead, at the bottom of the sea, in the scaly grasp of some sea monster. Because she couldn't rightly recollect how she'd gone from being rolled around in a dolly-tub under the waves to lying here, wherever here was.

'Like I has been put through the mangle on wash-day and hung out to dry,' she said to herself.

Then she gave herself a shake. 'Come on, girl, don't be a jobberknoll, the sun don't shine under the sea!'

But she still didn't want to look, so she put her hands up to her face and peered between her fingers, barely breathing. What she really dreaded, the fear she couldn't even give a name to in her head, was that the tiger was lying dead beside her.

She breathed deep. Through the gaps in her fingers she saw nothing but empty white sand and a wide beach, lapped by gentle waves. She swivelled round the other way, to get away from those waves.

'I never trusted that shummocky sea,' she muttered. 'And I were right, all along!' But there was nobody around for her to be able to say 'I told you so,' and it was no comfort anyway.

The beach was fringed by trees with long straight trunks and huge jaggedy leaves, each one as big as a branch, some drooping right down to the sand. She'd never seen trees like that at home. Beyond was the dense green darkness of a jungle – although Fly had no reason to know that was what it was called.

'It don't look much like Hyde Park, Stick,' she said, like she was writing him a letter home. Not that he'd be able to read it, even if she'd been able to write that much. And it wasn't like Stick had any regular address. She'd never be able to tell him now, any road. She was suddenly overwhelmingly sick of this adventure and longed to be back with the tumblers, going dimber-damber through the crowds, picking pockets on a Sunday afternoon.

At least by now she was pretty much sure she wasn't dead, so she took her hands away from her eyes and looked round properly. The beach was empty. Not a soul in sight. Fly had never been alone before. Not truly alone. There had always been someone there, in her crowded, chaotic life: scabby, snotty orphans fighting for scraps in the workhouse; Bill and his cough-drop of a wife shoving her up chimblies; gutterlings crowded round to hear her stories of an evening. And then her tiger . . .

She jumped up quickly to get away from the thought of the tiger and what might have happened to him, but her right leg was having none of it, and she promptly crumpled back on to the sand. She peered down.

'You ain't looking too clever,' Fly told her leg. It was swollen and bulging, with a raw, jagged cut, so she tore the sleeve off her new shirt – which didn't look so new now – and wound it round tight.

Wincing, she took a few steps across the sand to try it out. Her bare toes stumbled on what she thought at first was a black rock. But it was something soft, tangled in salt-stained black silk.

Fly slumped back down on to her bottom, and looked

around. The same pitiful little black hummocks were scattered all over the beach. They were bodies. The bodies of the silent servants, whose tongues had been cut out so they couldn't even cry for help as they drowned. She looked until she couldn't bear to look any more.

None of them would see their homes now. She had failed them, brave Zaliya and all those others who had trusted her to take them home. For a long moment, she could not move.

But she could not sit there for ever. 'Get up, Fly,' she whispered. 'You has to say goodbye.' It was the least a princess could do for her people.

She picked herself up and went slowly and painfully from one to another, touching each one lightly on the shoulder and counting them. But she'd never properly counted them before, so she didn't know if they were all there. Some of the crew were amongst them, including brave Barkus, with a thin trail of blood still trickling from his musket wounds. She couldn't bear to turn all the bodies over to look at their faces, but she knew that her faithful Zaliya was amongst them, because one head was entangled with strands of the long silky black hair which she had taken such pride in. Zaliya, whose name meant freedom.

'I'll come back and get you, and I'll take you back to your fambilies,' she promised, although she didn't know how she'd keep that promise, any more than she had when the tiger had made the same promise to the animals. 'And look how that's turned out,' she muttered. 'Some princess I've been, letting you all wind up dead on a beach.'

She was talking to herself, but she had to talk to someone. 'I has to get off this blasted beach, before I turns into a proper nutcase,' she muttered. 'And away from them blasted waves.' They looked as innocent as skipping lambs but the same waves a few hours before had ripped through the ship like a pack of wolves and torn the life out of all these people. Her people.

She turned her back on the sea and stumbled away up the beach. She was limping on both feet now, because the sand was scorching her bare soles like it was trying to roast her alive.

'If this place is home, I don't think much of it!' she muttered between clenched teeth. 'I reckon Jack were right. Barithea is a bad place.' But it hurt to think of Jack, almost as much as it hurt to think about her tiger, so she limped on.

There was a pile of rocks where the beach met the jungle, glistening with sea-spray in the sun like the rotting teeth of a sea monster. Setting her jaw, Fly managed to half-scramble, half-drag herself up to the highest point, in the hope of seeing someone else still living. But also in the dread of seeing her tiger dead. Or Jack.

'You ain't there!' she breathed in relief when she got to the top. As long as she couldn't see her tiger dead, she could believe in him alive. But what she did see was bad enough. The bodies of two of the zebras lay broken on the rocks, their manes caressed by a gentle sea-breeze that a few hours before had been a howling fury. A camel, with the same gloomy fiddle-face he'd had when he was alive, lay next to them like a discarded old sack. *He looks like he's saying 'I told you so'*, thought Fly. *Like he knew it would end badly all along*. One of the little golden monkeys she had last seen clinging, terrified, round Jack's neck, lay limp as a rag doll, floating in a rock pool. Its dead eyes were gazing up at the sun that it had been dancing in, just the day before.

It was too much.

'You was almost home!' she sobbed. She couldn't bear to look any more.

The sun was setting by the time Fly was able to lift her head from her damp knees. She stood up, leaning on the rocks for support, and looked out towards the horizon.

'Blast you! You devil!' she swore.

There was the ship with the black sails, still watching over the wreckage of the *Dark Destiny*, which it had done nothing to save as it sank. Barkus would never have taken them so close to the rocks, if it hadn't been for fear of that ship.

It was a good thing that Fly couldn't see the figure on board, who snapped his spy-glass shut with a snarl at that very moment.

'Damn her! The little brat is still alive.'

But some instinct told her it might be a good idea to get away from the beach – and away from whoever was on that ship.

She slid down to the rapidly cooling sand, landing on her good leg, and looked doubtfully into the thick jungle. 'No way is I going in there in the dark.' An evening chorus of rapid chattering and low growls and wild shrieks had started up amongst the trees, and there was no knowing what she would have to face once she stepped into that jungle. Better to wait 'til there was light so at least she'd be able to see what was lurking in there. 'But where can I kip? I needs a crib somewhere, away from them waves.' Jack had told her about the tide's sneaky habit of going up and down, and she didn't trust the sea not to creep back in and have another go at drowning her during the night.

Long shadows from the jagged rocks were falling dark on to the beach, and the white sand was tinged pink from the setting sun. But there was a glow coming from behind one of rocks at the back of the beach that had nothing to do with the sunset. Fly unconsciously patted at the belt of her britches before following the light. The tattered old metal box had somehow survived the storm and was still tucked safely in there.

Behind the rock there was a new horror waiting. It was the body of the captain, his hook hand stretched out and dug deep into the sand, as if he had died trying to reach something that mattered to him more than life itself. There was a look of agony on his hatchet face, his eyes locked on the ruby, which was nestled in a crevice, just out of his grasp, like it was taunting him.

'There you is!'

As she picked the ruby up, a flame leaped inside it, like it had recognised her and was glad, and she couldn't stop her own heart leaping in reply, in spite of everything she knew about it. She held it for a few moments. It was like being frazzled by bottled lightning down the fairground; it was like the first time she had touched the tiger; it was like every wild helter-skelter gallop she'd ever taken on her tiger's back.

'Nga Ran . . .' she breathed. The flame at its core flickered again. 'My Tiger's Heart . . .' Every time she held it, she wanted it more, like the sweet seduction of the poppy syrup.

But as she uttered those words, she got a sudden, vivid picture of her tiger's face, the bright stripes knotting into a dark frown, his golden eyes fixed on her, his black lips curling in disapproval. She dropped the ruby like it had burned her, and covered her eyes so she could keep seeing that beloved face instead.

'I'd give all the mint sauce in London to have you here 'stead of that stupid old stone,' she whispered. 'And all the pies.' And then she lifted her head and howled. 'Tiger! Tiger! Where are you?'

But there was nothing but silence.

'You don't even have to come back to me!' she howled up to the sky. 'I just need to know you're still alive. Alive and free.'

There was still nothing but silence and the brightening evening stars. She was alone. Fly sighed and frowned back down on the ruby.

'What would *he* say I should do with you?' The ruby was still glowing and flickering at her in the last rays of the sunset. She thought for a moment. 'Well, you did get us here, even if you caused a shipwreck,' she said to the ruby. 'Never know when you might come in handy again.' Then she thought but she didn't say out loud, *And you're all I've got left now, any road.*

She picked the ruby up again, trying to ignore the sparks it sent through her, and sealed it back into its dull metal box. Then she tucked the box back under her waistband, before limping away to find a safe spot to curl up in for the coming night. The last thing she did before falling asleep was to feel for the scarlet feather that Zaliya had tucked in the pocket of her britches. It was still there. But this time it just reminded her of broken promises.

CHAPTER 18

Fly was woken by a shower of raindrops on her face, but when she stuck out her tongue to lick them off, they were as sweet as strawberry ice, like she'd tasted for the first time with the tumblers, up Hampstead Heath last summer. 'Croopus! I'm killed!' Sparrow had cried, clutching his jaw, and Spud had run around shouting as how the ice had got in amongst his teeth and he was tooth-ached all over. And the crowd was full of grumble and they wanted the ice-cream man locked up for selling such dangerous stuff.

'Remember when we had them ices?' Fly rolled over, laughing, to remind Stick, but then the pain in her leg and the sand in her britches reminded her that she wasn't curled up in a church doorway with the tumblers, on one of those nights that she'd slipped away from Black Bill's.

She was thousands of miles away on a beach with no tumblers and no tiger and no Jack. And no idea what to do next.

When she looked up to see where the strawberry rain was coming from, she discovered it wasn't rain at all. 'It's the birds!' she cried. 'You ain't dead!'

Her flock of rainbow birds was hovering over her head, dropping sweet water on to her face from their beaks. She waved at them and tasted it again, but now there was salt mixed with the sweetness.

She struggled to her feet. 'Lawks, I feels like I've been two rounds with a costermonger's cleaver!' Her bruised limbs had stiffened up overnight, and there wasn't a bit of her that didn't hurt.

She was taking a few experimental hops on her good foot, when a scarlet wing brushed against her crest of black hair, shortly followed by another. Another couple of birds tugged at Fly's shirt with their beaks. Then the birds flew a little way down the path that led into the jungle, before doubling back and tapping and tugging at her again.

'You wants me to go with you,' guessed Fly, taking a hop down the path.

The birds bobbed up and down delightedly, like they were nodding.

'Well, I needs to find some water and some prog, any road,' she told the birds. 'And there's nowt on this perishing beach.'

What I wouldn't give for a drop of lobscouse now! she thought, hobbling after the birds towards the trees.

At the edge of the jungle, she stopped to find a branch to use as a walking stick, but the moment she stopped the birds swooped down and dive-bombed her.

'Cor, you're in a right flim-flam about something!' Fly looked uneasily back at the beach; the birds' impatience was catching. There was no sign of the ship with black sails this morning, but that didn't make her feel any better. Could the birds see something – or someone – coming after her?

'Best mizzle, girl,' she advised herself. 'Whoever it is, I'll lay they're not chasing after you to offer you a nice cup of tea.'

Once Fly plunged into the dense jungle, she couldn't see the flock of birds overhead any more, but she could still hear them calling and squawking above the trees, and the sound helped her to follow the path in the dim greenish light. But after a couple of hours of limping, Fly's head was swimming with the pain in her leg, and from two days without food or water. She slumped down on to a fallen log, ignoring the impatient squawks of the birds overhead.

'Keep your feathers on!' she snapped at them. 'Even if

Old Scratch himself is coming after me, I still needs some chow!' She looked up to the trees like she was expecting to see Jack swinging down with a bowl, brim-full of lobscouse.

'Ouch!' A large orange fruit fell on Fly's head and split apart, covering her face and hair with its sticky flesh. She gave her cheek an experimental lick. It was as good as the strawberry ice the birds had woken her with that morning. Seeing she liked it, the birds bombarded her with ripe fruit until she yelled up at them, 'Stop! Too much chow!'

'I dunno why I thinks they talk Pidgin,' she muttered to herself, trying to wipe the sticky juice off her skin. 'Unless all birds speak Pidgin . . .' In spite of the pain she was in, she grinned. 'You'd like that one!' she said, remembering the look on the tiger's face when he made the joke about the camels, but then her eyes started stinging and she had to blink hard.

Seeing she'd eaten enough, the cloud of birds swooped down to force her to her feet again, and urged her back on to the path that stretched ahead through the endless jungle.

Fly limped on for hours, trying to keep the weight off her bad leg with her walking stick, and hearing nothing but the cries of the birds overhead and the occasional grunt from some beast in the undergrowth. Sometimes she thought she heard something following her, and she forced herself to go faster, but all the skills of the old Fly, dodging the crushers along the city alleyways, were useless here. She had no idea where she could hide, and she'd never be able to run anyway with her bad leg.

'Blister these flies!' She'd started to stumble, swatting at the insects that were buzzing around her feverish face, filthy with sweat and mango juice. She jumped at the sound of a voice, before realising it was just her own, muttering an almost continuous string of gobbledegook.

She closed her eyes and felt the warmth of the tiger's flank pressing against her leg. He was growling. 'Have courage, girl!'

'You not making much sense, Fly,' she said to herself sternly, forcing her eyes back open. 'He's not here.' Then she made herself say it: 'He's drowndead. He's at the bottom of the sea.' In all her hungry years in the gutter, Fly had never felt emptiness like this.

It was evening when she finally emerged from the jungle to find a sweeping river, its rippled surface burnished to copper by the sinking sun, stretching out in front of her. It was so wide she could hardly make out the opposite shore. She crawled the last few steps through the mud and fell into the shallows, gulping down cool water to soothe her fever and her thirst.

A rainbow of birds flew down and settled in the water beside her, dipping their long beaks and swallowing it greedily down their dazzling throats.

Fly's leg was throbbing unbearably by now. 'Let's have a look at you,' Fly said wearily. She unwrapped the bandage, which was stained with stuff she didn't want to look at too closely. 'Drabbit it, I don't reckon as you should be that colour!' She stuck her leg under the water and lay back on her elbows to look over the river, letting the cold current numb the pain.

Away in the distance she could see snow-topped mountains soaring above green-clothed hills, and though she couldn't see them, somehow she knew there were crystal waterfalls tumbling down the mountains to join the river.

I've seen this place before, she thought, as she crawled away to sleep in a hollow in the riverbank. But then she gave herself another good talking-to, because she'd spent the afternoon chatting to a dead tiger, and somebody had to tell her to get a grip. *Don't be daft, girl. Stick would say you're going soft in the crumpet!*

Because how could she have been here before? Except perhaps in a poppy-syrup dream.

CHAPTER 19

Fly was shaken awake next morning by a rumbling in the earth, like the number 10 omnibus was crashing out of the jungle behind her. She lay still in the hollow, her eyes open, sweating with fever and fear.

There was no sign of the birds. She was completely alone, and she knew she couldn't run on her gammy leg. There was no exit but the dawn-pink river ahead of her.

'Blister me!' she swore. 'I ain't getting back into no tarnation water!'

But the rumbling kept coming, and as it got closer, she realised it was footfalls, so heavy they were shaking the earth. They were heading straight towards her, even though she'd hoped she was well hidden in her hollow. Whatever it was, it knew she was there. Deep down, she feared that the golem had smelled her out. But then she thought what the tiger would do, and hauled herself up to her feet to face the fear.

'It's the jumbos!' she cried, and in a moment, a long grey trunk was wrapped tight round her waist and she was being swung up to the shoulders of the largest elephant, the one that had rescued her from the fat man back on the docks.

'Thank you, thank you!' She bent down and kissed it where a little curl of hair fell forward on to its wide forehead. In reply, it filled its trunk and squirted a morning shower of cold river-water down on her head. Laughing seemed a strange thing to do, but it came back as easy as breathing.

Above her head, the birds were circling in delight at their own cleverness at finding the elephants, and the two younger elephants were crowding round, touching Fly with their trunks.

'You ain't drowndead! You ain't drowndead!' Fly cried, while they stroked her face with the tips of their trunks, as delicate as kisses. In her heart she was saying, *If the jumbos ain't drowndead, maybe he's alive too!* But she knew that she couldn't ask them, because it was only the tiger that could talk.

The joy didn't last long. The birds were soon twittering with impatience, flying ahead along the riverbank, and the elephants were just as jumpy as they followed at a rolling pace. They were continually looking back, trumpeting anxiously to one another.

'Why is you all in such a tweak?' gasped Fly, clinging to the flaps of the elephant's ears. 'I thought as you'd be happy, now you're free . . .'

And then it came to her, like a cloud over the sun or a blanket over a bird's cage. 'You still ain't safe, even though I brought you home . . . that's why you is still scared!' They'd been captured once, and sent across the sea for the fat man to sell in London. What was to stop them being captured again? Even if the fat man was dead, the greed of the king would never be satisfied.

Barithea is a bad place! Jack's warning echoed in her ears. It made sense now, as she smelled the fear rising from the hide of the elephant. A few weeks before, it had been cowering in the back of a cage. She wasn't going to let anyone take away its freedom again. *End this wickedness* – that's what Dalit had told her. Her hand closed round the metal box that hid the ruby. *Use it wisely* . . . the tiger had said. It was all she had left.

The elephants were climbing now, and she had to bend forwards and cling on with her knees as the path rose steeply above the river. Below, the rising sun had painted a golden arrow on the water, like it was pointing the way.

Fly peered ahead, through the thick heat haze which hung between the sheer red-earth cliffs, hiding what lay beyond the next wide loop. The birds swooped on, chattering with what now sounded less like fear and more like excitement. She leaned forward eagerly; it was like the birds had got into her belly.

And then she saw it. A golden cage, impossible in its delicacy, dangling over the river like a shining bauble. Tall trees drooped weeping branches towards it, as if to shelter it from the heat of the sun. Beyond the cage, in the distance, lay a shining city of milk-white marble domes, rising like translucent puffs of clouds into the perfect blue of the sky.

'Blimey!' Fly whistled between her teeth. 'That must be some parrot, to have a cage like that.' But she knew it wasn't a parrot in there, because she'd seen that cage before in her poppy-syrup dreams. And her heart wouldn't be pumping like this for no parrot.

Is my face clean? was the only thing Fly could think, after the elephant had swung her down and she stood on the top of the cliff above the river, looking towards the cage. The tiger would have told her. The tiger would have licked her clean with his rough tongue, rather than let his princess meet her father the king for the first time with a dirty face. But the tiger wasn't here, so she had to spit on her remaining sleeve and scrub her face with it, and hope that would do.

And after all, a dirty face wasn't the biggest problem standing between her and her father. The river was so wide, she couldn't even see for certain sure what was inside the golden cage. She looked up at the elaborate system of ropes that kept it suspended over the river; they were anchored by metal rings to rocks on each side of the gorge. Then she looked down at the deep waters of the river below.

Her head swam and she had to put her hand back to hold on to the elephant's thick leg. 'If I takes a tumble, I ends up in the drink again.' She shivered. She'd survived one drowning. But the ache in her heart reminded her that the tiger was more than likely drowndead. And Jack was more than likely drowndead. And if she fell into that river, she'd more than likely wake up drowndead too.

Fly edged closer to the ropes and examined them closely. She'd always liked a bit of daring and flying-by-the-seat-of-her-pants, but even she knew this was the most dangerous thing she'd ever done. 'I ain't afeard . . .' she muttered to herself and then she heard Jack's voice in her head. *It's just like rigging. Hold your gab, and listen. I'll show you.*

The air shimmered around her as she stepped on to one of the thick ropes and edged forwards like a circus tight-rope walker. Her arms were clinging to the supporting ropes, which spun a kind of web around the cage. She wondered if her uncle could see his brother's cage from the windows of his palace. *He's been watching him die, like a spider with a bluebottle,* thought Fly. *All for that perishing ruby!* It wasn't just the pain from her bad leg that was making her grit her teeth.

Just slide your foot, Jack's voice told her, in her head. *Nice and easy!*

'Nice and easy for you!' snapped Fly. 'You ain't the one up hanging up here like a nick-ninny!'

But then she was sorry she had snapped at him, because half-way across, Jack's voice stopped talking to her. In fact, she couldn't hear him in her head any more because the fear was drowning him out. She froze, unable to take another step. But it was just as far to go back as it was to go forwards.

The panic was at her throat, it was in her chest, like a wild beast. It was like that time she got trapped in the chimney, except this time it wasn't solid bricks around her, but shimmering air. Nothing to bind her to life, nothing to stop her falling . . .

She could see nothing either side of her. If she moved her head, she knew she would lose her balance and plunge into the ravine.

She couldn't look back. No way could the elephants help her now.

She couldn't look ahead, because part of the fear was about what was waiting for her in that golden cage. She still couldn't make out what was inside. She might be undertaking this nightmare journey only to find a dead father at the end of it.

He cannot last much longer, the fat man had said, and that was weeks ago. How many years had he been imprisoned here, alone with his despair? Looking down on his lost city, mourning his lost daughter, his ruined country. How long could anyone – even a king – survive like that?

Something kept telling her to look down, to let go, but she knew that if she did look down, her body would follow, sure as eggs is eggs. How long would it take to fall, when the only thing to look forward to was death?

'Jack!' she called, in desperation, her eyes screwed shut. 'Jack! Help me!'

Hold on, child! His voice came back to her. *Help is coming! Look!*

It was the chattering sound that gave her the courage to open her eyes. Ahead of her, dancing towards the cage from the other side of the river, was a mischief of golden monkeys. The sun sparkled on the fine hair of their coats so each one looked like a miniature sun, dazzling against the blue of the sky.

Then she remembered the poppy-syrup dream, in which

golden monkeys had kept the king alive by feeding him figs. And at last she dared to look at the cage. A cloud of scarlet hummingbirds was hanging in a haze around it.

'They is bringing him sugar-water! They wouldn't do that for a dead man!'

Fly took a deep breath and inched forwards, forcing herself to forget the empty air below her and focus on how she was going to tumble the lock and open that long-closed cage.

Perhaps she had dreamed this moment before, in a dream she'd never let herself remember. But this time it was real.

And then, the words, never heard before: 'Daughter! My lost daughter!'

The name, never heard before: 'Rahani!'

The forgotten face of a father, wild-bearded and burned black by the sun, but softened with love.

The exiled king, struggling to sit tall, but bowed by grief and guilt and pain.

And the chattering of monkeys and the chirruping of a hundred hummingbirds, cloaking the cage with gold and scarlet, to keep this reunion of father and daughter hidden from evil eyes.

CHAPTER 20

It was the terrified trumpeting of the elephants from the cliff edge that brought Fly back from the dream that had become a very strange reality.

'You have a face shaped like a heart,' her father had just told her, reaching out a wondering hand to stroke her cheek. His hand was bony as a bird's foot. It looked like a puff of wind would blow him to dust. 'You are the image of your mother.'

'I had a mother?' Fly gaped at him. 'Me?'

'Of course you had a mother, child!'

Fly could see him wondering what sort of education she'd had. *And it wouldn't take long to tell him about that,* she thought.

'Everyone has a mother, and a father . . .'

'Not where I come from,' muttered Fly, but perhaps he didn't need to know about the gutters where she'd grown up, just yet.

'She died when you . . .' He hesitated. 'She died before you were a year old. But it was grief over the war that killed her . . . grief over the treachery of my brother . . .' His voice faded, thin as tissue from want of use. 'Perhaps it was better that she died . . .'

'Did she call me – that – what's that name again?'

'Rahani.' Her father's face was overgrown with beard and wild grey hair, but she could see his eyes were brimfull. 'It means "soft and beautiful".'

Fly snorted. 'Not sure that suits me too well, Pa,' she said. 'I'll stick to Fly if you don't mind.'

He'd nodded, because he was just starting to get to know this daughter he hadn't seen since she was in her cradle, and everything about her was wonderful to him.

Mebbe best not tell him what Black Bill really called me, Fly thought to herself.

She had begun to contemplate quietly what to do next. *How the blue blazes is we going to get back across there?* She knew she couldn't ask him. It was more like becoming a mother than finding a father.

I wish Stick was here. Or Jack. Or you, Fly told the tiger, in her head. *Although, no disrespect*, she added, *but I'm not sure as a full-grown tiger would be much use in this particular boat of pickles.* The way the rope that suspended the cage was creaking, she and her father might, any moment, end up in the river anyway. *Another right pandalorum you've got yourself into, girl,* she thought to herself. *Not too many exits here.*

But then came the terrified trumpeting from the cliff edge, and Fly's flock of birds came shrieking towards the cage. Fly unwrapped her arms from her pa and stood up to see what was happening.

The jumbos were teetering on the cliff edge, backing away from a group of men with guns.

And at the centre of the group was a dead man.

Or at least, the man she had believed was dead. The last time she had seen him he was being sucked under the *Dark Destiny*, pulled down by Dalit. But even from this distance, there was no doubt in her mind that it was the fat man. The golem had smelled her out again.

'No! Jumbos!' Fly shouted. She could see what was in their minds. They were going to throw themselves off the cliff edge, rather than face the chains that the men were trying to fasten about their feet. 'Jumbos! Don't!' she cried. 'Let him take you! I promise I'll set you free!'

'Mighty fond of making promises you'll never be able to keep, girl,' she muttered, remembering all her broken promises – to Zaliya and her people, and to her animals left dead on the beach.

The elephants heard her, and stopped backing towards the edge. The men scurried round them, fastening chains around their feet. With a soft, resigned trumpeting that broke Fly's heart, they bowed their heads and let themselves be chained. 'They looks like the jumbos on that coat of harms on his trot-box,' remembered Fly. 'I always hated that coat of harms.'

Then she stood up against the bars and bellowed, 'My father is the king – and he says you're to let his animals go!' It was worth a try. Her father struggled to his feet beside her, but she could see the effort it took him to pull himself up.

The fat man laughed that high-pitched tinkling laugh. 'Your father is no longer a king, to be able to give such commands. His brother is the king. And you are nothing but a dirty little guttersnipe. All I need to do is to cut this rope . . .' He pointed at one of the thick ropes, fastened to an iron ring anchored in the cliff. '. . . and both you and your nobody of a father will die down there in the river.'

'My brother would not allow such evil!' her father shouted. 'This is a sacred river!' His bony frame rattled like a bottle of dried peas.

Fly was pretty sure that the fat man didn't much care about stuff like sacred rivers, after all the evil he had done, and she was certain sure her uncle wouldn't care neither, but then she almost laughed, because the fat man did take a step backwards. *What hokum!* she thought, because it looked like any other river to her. But it bought her a little time.

She turned her back on the fat man and was about to pull the metal box out of her waistband when her father stopped her hand.

'What do you have in there, daughter?' He had a curious look on his face.

'It is the ruby,' she said. 'The *Nga Ran*.'

Her father's face clouded and contorted into something she didn't much like the look of.

'How did you come by the Heart of the Tiger?' he demanded. 'My brother and I went to war for that ruby . . . he stole it from me . . . it was the most precious thing I ever owned . . .'

Fly wondered about that, and how losing it compared with losing a daughter. Or a wife. She shrugged. 'It were in the basket I were left in, at the workhouse.'

'I must see it!' Her father reached out greedily for the box.

The minute he heard about the ruby he was as betwaddled as the rest of them, Fly thought. *If I opens it here, and he makes a grab for it, we loses it anyways, and then we has got no ways to do a deal.*

'Not yet, Pa,' she said gently. 'We needs to save our skins first!'

Her father seemed to accept that, like a child being told it must wait for Christmas. But it had made her think.

I needs to trick that evil scorcher into getting us out of this rickety old bird-cage, she told herself. *Always look for the exit, girl.* So, still with her back turned, she tucked the box into her waistband before looking back to shout across the river again.

'I knows where the ruby is,' she called to the fat man.

'Where is it?' he replied quickly in that thin, high voice. 'Do you have it there?'

'Do you think I'm a complete clod-pate?' Fly shouted back. 'I hid it – I was afraid some dicey cove might try and nobble it. Some dicey cove like you!'

Fly continued, 'Bring us safe to the side, and I'll tell you where it is. But no havey-shavey business – or you'll never clap eyes on it again. And your precious king will know who to blame if he loses his precious ruby.'

The fat man gestured impatiently to the men who had been busy chaining the elephants together, and they turned their attention instead to the complicated system of pulleys and ropes that held the cage above the river.

Croopus, does they know what they're doing? wondered Fly, as they began to pull on one of the ropes and the cage started to sway and lurch, until she feared they might slip out between the bars. She sat down quickly and held her father close. He was shaking. *Lawksamussey, I hopes he don't go clean off his noddle . . .*

Fly's birds hovered anxiously overhead as the cage made its slow swoops and heart-stopping jerks across the void, until finally it bumped against the cliff edge. Some of the men scrambled down to help Fly and her father, who was now muttering incoherently, out of the cage.

'Take care of him,' she begged. 'He's as weak as a kitten.' The men looked up at her with wet eyes. *Croopus! Why they got the woefuls?* wondered Fly, watching them put their arms gently around him, and carry him carefully up the bank. And then she twigged. *They know who he is. They know he's their real king.*

The men looked away quickly to hide their tears when the fat man waddled up. 'Take him over to the elephants!' he ordered.

Fly staggered. Her knees had turned to junket as soon as she felt his evil bearing down on her once more. She knew the golem was creeping closer. *Do not let it in!* the tiger had told her. This would be the first time she had tried to face them both down, without the tiger beside her.

She took a deep breath. 'Why the devil is you not dead?' she demanded.

'You never did have any manners, did you, guttersnipe?' The fat man smirked. 'That pathetic traitor could never have had the strength to kill me – I snapped his neck like a matchstick!'

Fly shuddered. Poor loyal Dalit, putting up with this toad for so long, just to keep her safe. And she had always thought he was as evil as his master.

The fat man was oozing on. 'I discovered almost too late that he had plotted against me from the start. I started to suspect him when I found that the ruby had been left with you.' His laugh rippled through the layers of blubber beneath his robes. 'Without that ruby, you are nothing – how could anyone ever believe that sewer-scum like you could be a princess?'

Up 'til now, Fly would have pretty much agreed with him, but hearing him say it made her think for the first time that she wanted to give the whole princess thing a go. Just to prove him wrong.

'Now, where is it?' he snapped.

Fly shrugged, to buy herself time, and because she remembered how much he hated it. 'I dunno.'

She was concentrating on using every bit of strength she had to put the stares on him, to hide the telltale shape of the metal box in her waistband. But she'd never been strong enough to use her powers against him before. Surely it was only a matter of time before he twigged.

He stepped closer and she backed away, trying to remember how many footsteps it was to the cliff edge. 'Don't be impertinent, you filthy slum-spawn. Tell me where the ruby is!'

So he couldn't see it. Her stares were working.

'I dunno.' She shrugged again, and grinned in spite of the fear when she saw his vile toad-face bulge in fury.

But she stopped grinning when he darted at her and seized her by the shirt-collar. The men were watching open-mouthed in horror and she could have sworn she heard a whisper: 'Princess . . . give him the ruby!' But without the ruby, she and Pa were dead meat.

'Where is the ruby?' His vast bulk was pressing down on her, his foul snake-breath hot on her face, but her stares were still holding.

'I dunno,' she gasped. 'I don't rightly recollect.'

217

The fat man took another step, backing her towards the cliff edge. 'You are resisting me, with your pathetic powers,' he whined, tightening his grip on her collar.

Then he gave her a shake, and her feet were dangling over the cliff edge. 'Now – tell me!'

The only thing between Fly and death was the shirt Zaliya had stitched for her. *I hopes you sewed it good and tight, girl!* she thought.

'I ain't telling you, mister!' Fly gasped out. 'You're a devil! You watched that ship sink, and all them people die. You let my tiger drown!' The hatred welled up in her and she spat in the fat man's face.

It was almost the last thing she ever did. The fat man dropped his grip on her collar in disgust, and she fell backwards, clutching at the air. There was a groan from the men watching. Her hands snatched desperately for the cliff edge, and she was left dangling by her fingertips.

The fat man lifted one of his dainty feet, poised to crush her hands.

'Tell me, you little fool!' But his fleshy face was writhing with indecision. He knew if she fell, the ruby was lost for ever.

'If you don't pull me up, you'll never get the ruby!' she panted. 'Take us to my uncle, and I'll tell him, because he is royal, like me. Princesses don't do deals with the likes of you.'

You'd have been right proud of me, Fly told the tiger in her head, holding her father steady on top of her elephant as they lurched away at a rattling pace along the long sandy-red track leading from the river. *But that ain't much comfort if Pa and me has kicked the bucket by the morning*, she thought.

She had won her small victory over the fat man, who had finally turned away from the cliff, saying, 'No matter. Your uncle has something in his possession that will loosen your tongue.' Then he'd snarled at the men, 'Pull her up and tie her on the elephant with her father.'

Now he was riding ahead of them, taking out his fury and frustration by beating his own broken-spirited elephant with his stick. She had kept the ruby hidden with her stares. And she had kept herself and her father alive. But they were still his prisoners, being taken to face the brother who had robbed her father of his throne, the uncle who wanted her dead.

Beneath her, her elephant was stumbling, its long easy stride hobbled by the chains around its feet. Behind them, the two younger elephants were clinging to one another, trunk to tail, trying to keep up as the chains bit into their own legs. Fly could feel their terror and misery at being captive once more.

She looked about her. This country – Barithea – was supposed to be her home, but it was all so strange to her. Above her head, the birds were crying to one another, flying high in the sky to keep out of reach of the fat man and his nets. She peered into the thick undergrowth, where the jungle had been hacked back; there was a constant rustling in the darkness, as if an army of animals might be gathering there, but she could see nothing. No beast would dare show itself around the fat man. *A bad place* . . . That's what Jack had said. And he was right.

She felt no better about Barithea once they entered the city walls. The beauty of those milk-white, translucent domes that Fly had seen floating in the distance was marred by the filth of the squalid little shacks that squatted around them. The gutters stank, sluggish and festering with rats and rubbish. But she knew she would feel more at home there, amongst the poor who grubbed a living in the shadow of those shining domes, than in the glistening palace up ahead.

Any children playing in the fetid gutters were snatched inside as soon as their mothers saw the fat man. The streets emptied; those who had been out and about scurried away down dark alleyways, before they could be seen. The fear of the fat man and his master – the king – was everywhere, like a sickness.

'Why is they all so scared?' Fly whispered to her father. But he did not reply, because he was still floating high above the sacred river. His mind seemed to have snapped the moment he stepped foot on the earth. Perhaps it could not bear the shock of too much reality, after so many years with nothing but those golden monkeys and scarlet birds for company.

Fly reached out and patted his withered hand. 'Pa?' He smiled gently, but he didn't know her. Perhaps his mind would never mend. And she would never really get to know her father, even now she had finally found him.

CHAPTER 21

'Croopus, ain't this a weaselly welcome for a princess!' Fly picked herself up off the floor and sniffed. 'It stinks like a haddock's armpit down here!'

She and her father had been thrown unceremoniously down a flight of stone steps into a damp dungeon that stank like the previous occupant had dragged himself into a corner and died of despair.

'I ain't smelled nowt as bad as this since Stick and me hid down the sewers after we'd prigged that piglet. Don't rightly know what we thought we was going to do with it!' She snorted at the memory of that piglet squealing away down the tunnel, and then she thought perhaps she shouldn't have shared that memory with her pa. But he was still lost in another world, muttering and singing to himself, songs from a happier time. *Best off not knowing where he is*, thought Fly, as she set about trying to find something soft to lay him down on.

In the dim light begrudged by a small barred window, she discovered what looked like a pile of sacking in a corner, but when she pulled at it, it stirred and yelled at her. 'What the devil! What you doing? This is my bed!' And it snatched the sacking back and wrapped it tight round itself again, growling at her like a street-cur.

'Jack?' Fly said, cautiously, because he looked like he might bite her.

'Child!' Jack sprang up, discarding his precious sack, and threw his thin arms around her. She couldn't remember ever having been hugged like that, but Fly was always one to catch on quick, and she hugged him back, just as tight. 'I thought you was dead!'

'Me too!' Fly could hardly breathe, he was holding her so tight. 'And I soon will be, if you don't leave off strangling me!'

He released his hold on her, laughing, and stood back to peer at her. 'What happened – what you doing in this place?'

'I woke up on the beach – the birds found me . . .'

'I told you the birds loved you.' Jack nodded.

'They showed me the way . . . and the jumbos came too . . . and I found my Pa . . .'

'Pa – what d'you mean, Pa?' Jack said quickly. 'No! You're the same as me! No father, no mother – that's what you said!' He sounded really angry, like he thought she'd lied to him.

'I tried to tell you, on the ship,' Fly said quickly. 'But it sounded like such a load of moonshine. It turns out I'm a princess – and my pa, he was the king, but I didn't know until I found him. Any road, my uncle stole his kingdom – and the ruby . . .'

'I know that story! They are bad men, your father and uncle! They killed so many men, just for that ruby.' Jack's face was dark with anger. 'Why would brothers go to war with each other for a ruby?' He spat on the floor in disgust.

It wasn't often Fly had nothing to say. But she couldn't help agreeing with Jack. She remembered the look on her father's face when he found out she had the ruby, and she hadn't much liked the look of it.

In the end she asked, 'What about you? How come you is in chokey?'

'When the mast broke, I went almost to the bottom of the sea . . . my poor little monkey drowned . . .' He stopped, like he'd run out of words. Then, 'It was almost sun-go-down time by the time I swam to the port, but the soldiers caught me and put me in quod.'

'So they has locked you up down here for doing nothing? Not for prigging nowt, or dipping pockets or nothing?' Fly knew that in London they'd hang a gutterling any chance they got, but it looked like there wasn't even London justice here.

Jack shook his head. 'I told you, it's a bad country. They said I was a spy – and they'll hang me or sell me as a slave.'

'Mebbe if I gives my uncle the ruby, he'll let you go . . .' said Fly, half to herself.

'You have the ruby?' Jack looked even angrier. 'What the devil do you want with the ruby?'

'Keep your hair on! I ain't going to keep it!' protested Fly quickly. 'But they is all so doolally for it, I reckon it could get us out of pokey!'

'Daughter! Are you there?' came a quavering call. Her father had remembered he had a daughter.

'Yes, Pa!' Fly hurried back to his side. Her insides flipped and turned to junket when he smiled up at her. Whatever she thought about the wrongs the ruby had driven him to, he was still her father, and she'd never had one before. But by the looks of him, she wouldn't have one for much longer.

Jack followed her more slowly, and watched while she propped the sick man gently up against the wall of the dungeon, and looked about for some way of making him comfortable.

'Take my bed,' Jack said, and he tossed his sack down on the floor beside her father. 'Here . . .' He kneeled down and helped Fly to lift the old man up, and settle him on the rough sacking. But Jack looked away, scowling, when she smoothed her father's bedraggled grey hair from his face and kissed him good night.

During that dark night Fly dreamed she heard her tiger roaring. It was a rib-rattling roar that shook the stones of the dungeon and echoed around the hole he'd left in her heart. The roar woke her up because it seemed so real.

But all was quiet, apart from Jack's loud snores and her father's faint breath. *At least Pa's still breathing*, she thought. *He ain't stuck his spoon in the wall just yet.*

Fly sighed as she tried to settle back on the hard stone. But every time she shut her eyes, the tiger was pacing through the darkness behind her closed lids, gold glinting on black, and the soft weight of his paws trod heavy on her dreams.

Fly had never seen riches like this, but to be fair to her, not many people outside this palace ever had. 'Blister me!' she muttered. 'Ain't this dandy!'

Every wall of the royal court was encrusted with emeralds and sapphires and garnets, patterned like a fossilised snake-skin. The floors were polished marble, veined with swirls of pinks and pale blue that looked like maps of imagined worlds. And the ceiling arched so high and blue overhead that it might have been the sky, except the sky cost nothing, and the blue of this lapis lazuli was beyond price.

'Bust me!' Fly swore softly. 'Ain't this just dandy?' Dandy was really the only word for it. But then she had to concentrate, because she and Jack were supporting her father, who was away in his own world again and could not walk alone.

She'd insisted when the guards had come to get them that Jack had to come too, in order to help carry her father. But the main thing that was occupying her was keeping the stares up, to stop every eye in the palace from seeing the ruby. It was there in its modest, tattered old box, tucked firmly into her waistband. Fly was still hoping it would buy them an exit.

It was a long walk down the hall, between courtiers dressed in flowing gowns of bright silks like those the fat man wore. A rumble went through the court as they passed, a rumble that sounded like astonishment, but Fly put it down to the sight of their old king, after so many years of believing he was dead.

At the end of the long walk, at the top of a flight of steps, stood a throne of burnished gold that looked very much, to Fly's mind, like a large coal scuttle. And perched in the golden coal scuttle, on cushions of crimson, was a puffed-up little man, so weighed down with bejewelled and bejangled robes and gold bangles that he looked like a hermit crab. *He looks like he's got stuck in a shell what's too small for him*, thought Fly.

It was her uncle, and he was watching all that was left of his family make their slow and painful progress towards him. *It must be a bit of a disappointment to him*, thought Fly, *after all the trouble he's took to get rid of us.*

When they reached the foot of the steps, someone scurried forwards with a chair and she turned her back on the man who called himself king, while she and Jack settled her father. It was a small act of defiance, but she didn't have much.

When finally she and Jack turned to look him in the eyes, her uncle's face was an ashen-grey beneath the dark skin they shared. He turned to the fat man, who was cringing at the foot of the steps, wringing his little hands. Fly had never seen the fat man look scared.

'What is the meaning of this? You told me only of the daughter! How is the son here, too?'

The rumble around the court turned into a roar. They had all seen the same thing, but hadn't dared say it out loud.

'Silence!' cried her uncle. 'I will have silence!' But though the roar died down, the rumble continued.

'Where did the son come from? You told me he was dead!'

Fly and Jack looked at one another over her father's head. Fly shrugged, and Jack shrugged too. Between them, her father stirred. His brother's voice had brought him back from wherever he had been. He looked up at Fly, and then he looked at Jack.

'My son? Rahinti?' It was a question, but Jack didn't know the answer, and nor did Fly.

'Father.' Fly kneeled in front of him, pulling Jack down to kneel beside her. 'Did I have a brother?'

'Your mother gave birth to twins . . . such a happy day . . . a double blessing, we said . . .' her father whispered. 'First a son – Rahinti – it means "pure of soul". And then a daughter – Rahani. She said you had faces like hearts . . .'

His frail arms reached out and he cupped a heart-shaped face in each hand. 'My children . . . my brother took you away from me, before he locked me in that cage . . . he said he would never let me out until I gave him the ruby, but I did not have it . . . I did not know where it had gone.'

Even as her father wept, Fly wondered for a moment which he had mourned more, his babies or the ruby.

'He told me you had both died . . . those were his last words before he left me there . . .'

A gasp went round the court.

'So that's why I was warned never to come to this country!' Jack turned to Fly. 'There was a letter left with me in the basket, at the orphan-place! It was the only thing left with me,' he muttered. 'Somebody was trying to keep me safe – to save me from him . . . from my own uncle!' He spat those last words out, glowering beneath his dark brows at the king.

'An end to this nonsense!' Their uncle levered himself out of his coal scuttle. 'My brother lost his claim to the throne many years ago – so whoever these filthy guttersnipes are, it is of no importance. I will have children of my own soon, when I am married . . .'

He leered at a girl in the court. She wasn't much older than Fly, and when the king looked at her, she looked like she was about to be sick. Then he turned and glared at Fly. 'The reason you were brought here was to deliver the ruby to us, the *Nga Ran*, which is mine by right. So where is it?'

Fly was still getting over the fact that she had a brother. Stick was the closest she'd ever had to a brother, and she'd thought when he'd waved her goodbye from the dockside, she would never have another. It felt like Jack was the thing she had been missing all her life. But she had to stop staring at him and think.

There was such misery and fear in this palace, she could feel it, just like she had out on the streets. These people didn't want this man as king, but they were too scared of him to do anything about it. She looked at Jack and he nodded at her. It was like when they had been working the rigging together, not needing words to know what the other one was thinking. This country was their country, their kingdom. It was up to them to put it right.

'Uncle,' she said slowly. 'If you had to choose, which would you keep? The ruby, or that there fancy gold bucket you is sitting in – the throne?'

'What nonsense is this? Why should I choose? The ruby is mine, and the throne is mine!'

'Blest if I can see any ruby, my cocky. Can you?' replied Fly, airily, confident now in the power of her stares. 'I is the one what knows where the ruby is. And you is the one what's got to choose. Ruby – or throne?'

'No, daughter!' Fly's father started up to his feet in protest, before collapsing back on to the chair. 'You cannot give the ruby away! It is beyond price!'

'Beyond what price, Pa?' blazed Fly, suddenly angrier than she'd ever been. 'Is it worth all the lives what have been lost? Is it worth more than your people, more than your animals? More than my ma – more than your children?' Jack took her hand. 'Me and Jack, we don't want no ruby, do we?'

'It is a bad ruby! It has brought nothing but evil,' Jack declared. 'You choose – the ruby or the kingdom!'

He and Fly threw down the challenge to their uncle. But their uncle swatted it away like a fly, with a contemptuous flick of his bejewelled hand. He smiled. It wasn't the kind of smile that had anything to do with happiness. 'I think we have something that will change your mind, guttersnipe,' he said to Fly, and nodded to the fat man. 'Bring it in!'

Snarling and impotent, a bedraggled but magnificent beast was hauled in chains from the doorway that led down to the dungeons.

It was the saddest sight Fly had ever seen, and she had seen a fair few in her short life. Fly thought her heart would break at that moment, and she let out a cry as she stepped forward, before being seized by two guards.

'No!'

The tiger's every powerful limb was fettered by chains, so his paws dragged with the effort of walking. A heavy iron collar chafed at his throat as he struggled to shift his weight between his mighty shoulders. The symmetry of the bright orange and black stripes of his thick coat was marred by bloody weals where he had been whipped. This creature had put up a fight for his freedom.

The tiger padded slowly but soundlessly up the long, marbled aisle. His golden eyes were fixed on the man who called himself king, his black pupils narrowed to pinpricks of contempt.

'Tiger!' Fly cried.

'My girl,' he growled in reply, and it was like a caress. 'My princess.'

'How did they catch you?'

'I came looking for you,' he replied. 'You didn't think I would leave you? I gave you my promise – to restore you to your throne.'

'But they caught you?' Jack joined in. Fly wasn't surprised. Deep down she had always known Jack would be able to speak tiger too; they shared it in their blood.

233

'Yes. They caught me again. And now you must end this wickedness, no matter how high the price. Our country has suffered for too long.'

Their uncle paled. He knew that Fly and Jack were talking to the tiger, though he plainly could not understand any of it. But the look on their father's face was quite different. It was a mixture of joy and deep envy, as he tried to follow the conversation. He reached out a trembling hand and touched Fly's face. 'You can talk to this beast, daughter?'

Fly nodded.

Her father's eyes filled with wonder. 'Our royal power to speak with tigers has been lost for many generations. In the old days our kingdom was called the Land of the Tiger . . . *Langa Ran*. But that name was forgotten long ago . . .'

Their uncle interrupted with an impatient clank of his gold-bangled arm. 'Talking to tigers? Ha! A mere party trick,' he sneered. 'It proves nothing. Now, which is it to be? The ruby – or the beast?'

Fly shook her head.

'Make up her mind.' He nodded to the fat man. 'The ruby, girl! Now! Or the tiger dies!'

Fly's tiger bared his white teeth and roared, the most rib-rattling, earth-shattering roar she had ever heard. It was a call to battle, and it rose up to the open arches above and out

234

beyond the palace, to the city streets and the jungle beyond, so that it seemed like the whole country must hear it.

The fat man snatched up a spear from one of the soldiers, and darted towards the tiger. The tiger leaped at him, but he fell back, snarling and impotent, still chained by every limb. The fat man laughed his tinkling, sneering laugh, because he knew he was in no danger. He pointed the spear towards the tiger, ready to strike, and the tiger roared again.

Fly remembered that bloody picture in her bedroom back in the fat man's house, of a dying tiger with a spear thrust deep into his heart and the bile rose in her throat.

'No!' she cried. 'Stop!'

CHAPTER 22

'You have a plan.' The low growl wasn't a question.

It was a sorry procession, back through the city towards the river. Fly and Jack were stumbling in chains, beside the shackled tiger, while their uncle led the way on the back of one of the elephants, in a litter, shielded from the heat of the sun by curtains of cloth-of-gold. Behind them, their father was being carried in a much more modest affair, but Fly knew he wouldn't be missing his children; after a brief spell of sanity, he was off in his own doolally world again. Somewhere at the back of the procession was the fat man, in disgrace over the reappearance of the royal twins who were supposed to be dead. She sensed the golem too was close by, still looking out for a chance to own her.

'Mebbe,' replied Fly, but it didn't carry much conviction. 'I've codded him into thinking the ruby's hidden near the river, close to the cage.'

'But it is in the waistband of your trousers.'

She nodded. There was no bamboozling the tiger. She never could put the stares on him.

'And what do we do when we get there?' asked the tiger.

Fly shrugged. She wasn't doing it to annoy any more. She just didn't know. There really was no exit this time. She and the tiger were both limping, Fly from her bad leg, and the tiger from where he had been beaten. She was feverish from the infected wound, and it was difficult to think straight, but it was clear, once they got to the river, that she would have to hand over the ruby, or the tiger would die. And then they'd all be killed anyway. Her new father and her new brother, when she'd only just found them. Why would her uncle keep any of them alive?

The tiger roared again. He'd been roaring all the way through the city, even though the soldiers who were guarding them beat him every time he roared. Fly thought she knew why he was doing it – it was all he had left, now they had taken away his freedom again – but she couldn't bear to see him hurt.

'Please stop roaring!' Fly begged, but he ignored her.

The sound of the tiger's roar was bringing faces to every window, though the streets remained as empty as they had been the day before. Fly waved, and she nudged Jack to do the same, because she remembered that old King Billy had never waved. If she was going to be a princess, even for a few hours, and this was going to be her only royal progress, she might as well make it good. But very few waved back.

'Why is they so scared?' Fly demanded, impatiently. 'Why don't they do something?'

'They're scared of our uncle,' said Jack, bitterly.

'And not everyone has your courage, girl,' added the tiger.

Jack added, 'They're weeping for all their children who were sent away as slaves.'

The tiger roared again.

Fly thought of all those pathetic little bundles, dead on the beach they had longed to set foot on once more. She'd never be able to go back for the bodies of Zaliya and the other servants now. She would never be able to give their bodies back to their families. Another broken promise.

But if Fly had looked back, she would have seen something very different from their journey to the city the day before, something that might have given her hope.

Behind the procession, hundreds of people were emptying out of their houses. They were following the sound of the tiger's roar.

All the way through the city, and out on to the long dusty road to the river, the tiger kept roaring, and kept getting beaten. Until at last Jack seized a stick from one of the men and brandished it at them.

'You cowards! Leave him – he ain't doing you any harm!'

And after that, the guards seemed happy to let the tiger roar.

It felt much further, back to the river. This time they had to walk every step, instead of being carried along by the elephants. 'Poor jumbos,' sighed Fly, watching her uncle whipping his elephant ahead of them. 'I promised as I'd set you free, and now look at you.'

She'd never be able to stop the animals being sent away to be sold again, never be able to stop the birds being snatched from the sky. The scarlet feather was still in her pocket, but she'd been holding it so tight for so long, it was in tatters. Like her promises.

But again, if she could have looked back now, Fly might have felt more hopeful.

All the animals that had remained hidden the day before as they had made their way to the palace were now creeping out to join the hundreds of silent people streaming out of the city. They too were being drawn by the roar of the tiger.

'Blister it!' Fly swore. 'There must be a way out!' She'd never failed to spot an exit in the past.

'You still have the ruby,' pointed out Jack. 'A man like that will do anything for that ruby. He would even die for that ruby.' He squinted at her in the bright sunlight. 'As long as you don't want the ruby for yourself.'

Fly was about to snap back at him, but something stopped her. Her hand strayed to the tattered box at her waistband. She was afraid that Jack was right. She feared that bit of her was still there, the bit that hankered after the thing that had caused all this horror. And she knew that every time she thought about the ruby, the golem drew closer to her.

'You want to keep the ruby, don't you?' a voice whispered, but she wasn't sure if it was the voice of the golem, or her own.

The tiger's golden eyes were steady on her, like he could see right through her. But she wasn't sure what he could see.

When they came to the river, the golden cage was dangling like a broken toy over the ravine. 'Tie my brother up,' barked her uncle, and her father was dragged towards the cliff edge.

All that gammon about the sacred river! thought Fly. *He's going to throw us all in, soon as I hand over the ruby.*

Fly and Jack stood side by side, the tiger between them, in front of their uncle. He had brought the golden coal scuttle with him, so that he could sit in state for the moment the ruby was restored to him. Fly saw Jack dig his fingers deep into the tiger's coat, just as she was doing, and she wondered if the sparks were flying up into his heart too.

'Seize the tiger!'

The tiger was dragged away from them, snarling, and the fat man stepped forward with the spear, ready to plunge it into the tiger's heart.

'Well? Where is the ruby?'

It was time to choose.

Fly could have pretended to find the ruby hidden in a heap of rocks, but it was more fun to watch the fury on the fat man's face as she pulled the metal box from her waistband. 'I had it in my kecks all along, see!' she taunted him.

'Open it!' gasped her uncle. 'Let me see it!'

The box fell open in two perfect halves and she held the ruby in her hands. It flickered at her in greeting.

Fly perfectly understood the greed in her uncle's face. She knew all about the tug of money; she'd not spent her childhood stealing to stop herself starving, without knowing that money meant the difference between life and death.

'Fly!' hissed Jack. She could see the doubt in his eyes, but the tiger made not a sound. He just looked at his princess with those steady golden eyes. There was a perfect stillness in the air, as if the wind itself was holding its breath.

Fly looked down at the ruby again, and back at her uncle's face. He'd never been so hungry he couldn't sleep. He'd never been so cold he'd cried. The greed in his eyes was nothing to do with the greed of a guttersnipe who just wanted to feed her people. And set her animals free.

'Here, Jack,' Fly said. 'I don't want it.' She winked at him. 'Catch!'

She tossed the ruby to her brother. It glinted for a moment in the air, before he caught it. Her uncle gasped and launched himself out of the coal scuttle to grab it from his nephew, and in the same moment the fat man dropped the spear and leaped towards the jewel he had always coveted for himself.

'I don't want it neither!' Jack grinned, and he tossed the ruby back at Fly, over the heads of the fat man and their uncle. They grabbed at it, but it was already safely back in Fly's hands.

Fly took a step closer to the cliff edge, and the two men followed her, never taking their eyes off the ruby. It glinted and winked at Fly, like it saw the joke and it was laughing too.

'Here!' She threw the ruby back again to Jack. It felt lighter each time she let go of it. The men whimpered with frustration as they stretched their arms for it and failed. They hadn't noticed that Jack had also taken a step closer to the ravine.

Fly was at the very edge when Jack tossed it back this time. 'Catch!'

'I told you – I don't want it!' Fly said for the very last time, and she batted the ruby away, over the cliff.

The whole crowd watched the ruby, and it felt like the Earth stopped turning to watch with them.

At first the ruby seemed to rise to greet the sun, as if it was enjoying its freedom at last, before starting its glittering descent towards the river.

And after it went her uncle and the fat man.

Their screams echoed off the red cliffs as they dropped down into the sacred river. The golem vanished after them.

'Daughter!' cried her father in horror. 'What have you done?' But from the tiger there was a low rumble of approval.

And behind Fly and Jack, that rumble was echoed and turned into a roar from the vast army of people and animals that had followed them to the cliff edge, in the hope of a better kingdom.

'Sorry, Pa!' Fly shrugged, and she grinned at her brother. She knew that whatever lay ahead, they would do it together.

EPILOGUE

'Sit still.'

'I can't sit still . . . I ain't never sat still this long before,' Fly grumbled. She and Jack had decided against the golden coal scuttle – and anyway, there was only one, which was no use for a sister and brother who were ruling their kingdom together. But it turned out that the ancient mahogany thrones of the Land of the Tiger – *Langa Ran* – were not very comfortable.

'You have never been a queen before,' replied the quiet voice of the tiger, beside her. He lay peaceably between the simple thrones on which she and Jack were sitting, his great head lifted proud from his paws to gaze out at the huge crowd gathered before them.

'Stop fidgeting, child,' hissed Jack.

Fly scowled. 'Who you calling child?'

'I was born first, remember!' Jack grinned, and Fly forgot to scowl and grinned back, because she had a brother. A new brother, she corrected herself, because Stick had been her brother too. But that was another life, and now she had to get used to this one. She stopped fidgeting and looked out at her people.

In front of her, on a funeral pyre of sweet-smelling wood, lay the bodies of the servants, wrapped now in shining white silk. Fly had insisted on collecting their bodies from the beach herself, accompanied only by her faithful elephants and a rainbow flock of whirling birds. Together they had brought Zaliya and the others back, and Fly had given each body to their weeping family. Now the people had gathered to say goodbye.

A single body, wrapped too in simple white silk, lay closer to Fly and Jack, ready to be laid on the funeral fire. It was the body of the father neither of them had ever known, except as a frail old man whose mind was broken by grief and suffering and – at the last moment – shame.

The ruby led me into evil. Forgive me, my children.

Those had been his last words. For their father's heart had failed after the ruby was carried away by the sacred river.

'It is time,' said the tiger now, and Fly and her brother

rose and together they picked up the light-as-a-feather stretcher and carried their father to join the other bodies on the funeral pyre.

Fly and Jack each took up a blazing torch and touched it to the wood. It crackled and sweet smoke rose as they backed away, bowing their heads in farewell.

The tiger came and stood between them and Fly twisted her fingers deep into his coat and felt the sparks fly up to her heart, just as the sparks of the fire were flying up to the blue sky.

'I knew from the first time I tasted your blood that you were the rightful queen of my country,' the tiger said. 'I didn't tell you, because I thought you might be afraid of the task ahead.'

'I ain't afeard of nothing!' Fly declared.

The tiger nodded. 'I know that now. But I knew I had to bring you home.'

'Gammon! It were me, bringing you home,' Fly objected, and then she stopped and laughed.

'That ruby . . .' she said.

'Yes?' The tiger raised an eyebrow. She'd never noticed he had eyebrows before.

'It didn't have no powers, after all, did it?'

'No,' replied the tiger. 'It was all gammon.' He grinned, and Fly grinned back.

'I'm going now,' he said.

'I have to let you go, don't I?' Fly asked, but it wasn't really a question. He nodded, and reached out a velveted paw and drew it gently across her heart. No claws this time. And there was no trace of doubt as he gazed at her with his golden eyes.

Then the tiger turned and the crowd parted as he padded silently away. But it seemed to Fly that the earth was shaking beneath his paws as he went.

Fly wanted to run after him and shout and scream and put her arms around his thick neck and hold him to her for ever, but she was a queen now and everyone was watching.

A touch came at her cheek and brushed away the wet stuff that was falling from her eyes. It was the elephant, the one that had whisked her on to the ship, and carried her safely to her father. He dried her face delicately with the tip of his trunk, and then he turned to follow the tiger.

Jack squeezed Fly's hand, and her eyes blurred as she looked out over the cheering crowd. Behind them, she could see all the other animals turning to leave, melting back into their land. Going home.

And she knew she had to let them all go. Because that's what it meant to be free.

AUTHOR'S NOTE ABOUT FLY'S WORLD

Fly inhabits a time-slip that's slid in somewhere between the rumble-tumble of the Georgians and the energy and inventiveness of the Victorians. That time-slip has allowed me the freedom to prig the best – and the worst – bits from different times, and to make up a lot more. I've been a bit like Spud, having an eye for the plummiest bits of a steamed pudding.

King Billy, with his hankersniff, is no king who ever ruled – but also every king or queen who ever ruled with more regard for the colour of their silk stockings than for the clothing of their people. Barithea is no country that ever existed – but also every country where people ever dreamed of overthrowing injustice and tyranny.

What *is* true is that thousands of children, like Fly's

gang of gutterlings, lived neglected and in terrible poverty on the streets of London. Hungry, filthy and grubbing a living from the gutters, with parents who were dead, or starving too.

Fly's tiger stepped out of the shadows of Jamrach's Animal Emporium – a kind of pet shop for exotic animals – which once stood on the Ratcliffe Highway near London's docks. Shiploads of beautiful creatures were unloaded here from all over the world and sold, mostly for the entertainment of rich fools who could afford to buy them and gawp at them behind bars, until they died of misery. A tiger once escaped from there, the story goes, and made a bid for freedom, but got entangled with a three-year-old boy in the street. Mr Jamrach forced the tiger's jaws open to free the boy and was hailed a hero.

It's not told what happened to the tiger. But he has escaped now, all these years later, to burn a bright path through the dark pages of Fly's story.

I hope you love him as much as Fly did. And as much as I do.

FLY'S GUIDE TO GUTTERLING

A

Adam and Eve's – don't rightly know who them Adam and Eve coves are – I ain't never met them – but mebbe they is in the habit of going round with no togs on. This means that you is bare-naked as the day you was born.

addlepated – to my mind, you can't have enough words for coves what are daft or stupid, 'cos the streets are full of them. Mostly it's on account of all the gin, what addles the few brains they was born with.

all rug – when a gutterling says summat is all rug, you knows it's all good and safe.

B

bags of mystery – we all loves a sausage – or a snossidge, as Spud calls them – but nobody rightly knows what's in them, and that's why they is called 'bags of mystery'. I wouldn't be surprised if a few of Pardiggle's donkeys have ended up in some of them.

bang-up – when summat is bang-up, it's prime, the best ever.

barmy – I told you that us gutterlings has a lot of words for coves what are soft in the head.

bloaters – this is a sort of fish. You ain't never far from the smell of fish in London. Oftentimes they don't smell too good, 'cos mostly it's been a while since they saw the sea. But I is partial to a twist of fried fish, when I can prig a bit off the back of a stall.

blue devils – it's the blue devils what gets you when you're feeling a bit down. Dunno why they is blue, but it's as good a colour as any when you got the mulligrubs and you is feeling miserable.

bobbery – this is ship-talk for trouble and botheration.

bonce – you needs a few words for your head, where I comes from, 'cos it's a rare day when someone don't beat you over the bonce, or gives you a clip round the ear, for nothing – or less.

bow-wow mutton – this is where the mystery comes in when it comes to them sausages. Mostly when they says they is made of mutton, or sheep, it's more likely to be some stray dog what's been drowndead in the Thames.

brown bread – dead. This is another thing what you needs a lot of words for when you lives in the gutters, 'cos plenty of gutterlings end up that way.

buff it – this is what them coves Adam and Eve likes to do. When they takes all their togs off, they're buffing it. It don't take long for a gutterling to buff it, 'cos there ain't never much to take off.

bunkum – a load of old rubbish.

C

to case a joint – this is when you is poking round a place to find the best way in without getting caught.

chimbley – I is quite the expert on these, 'cos I has spent most of my days inside them and I knows all their nasty tricks –wide ones and narrow ones and ones what seem to go on for ever and it feels like you ain't never going to get to the top. Toffs call them chimneys, but I reckon that whatever you calls them, a chimbley is pretty much the same as what the preachers call Hell. Dark and hot, with some devil poking you up the backside to make you go faster.

chin-wagging – this is what me and the gutterlings does, on the nights I gives Black Bill the slip, when we all sits round and tells stories.

chokey – we has lots of words for prison, 'cos mostly a gutterling's day is spent trying to prig some prog or dip some pockets without the crushers nabbing us and locking us up. Once you is in chokey, there's only two ways out – transportation to 'Stralia or being strung up on the gallows. That's if you don't croak first.

chuckeroo – I reckon this is ship-speak for when you means a boy.

clod-pate – another of them useful words for all the fools we comes across on the streets.

cobbily-mash – nobody can tell me what's in this stew, but it smells pretty fishy.

to cod – us gutterlings are always on the look-out for ways to trick – or cod – someone out of a shilling or a sausage, but we're always on the lookout in case we get codded too. London is a place what's full of codders and codocity, and you have to have your wits about you to survive.

costermonger's cleaver – a costermonger is a cove what sells all sorts of stuff, but any right-thinking gutterling knows that they is the toughest, most curmudgeonly coves in the whole of London. They is always looking for a fight, and they oftentimes has a sharp cleaver handy, what they use for chopping up meat. You'd have to be barmy to cross them, 'cos you'll most likely end up brown bread.

cove – this word will do for any man you come across.

to croak – same as sticking your spoon in the wall or brown bread – it means you is dead.

crushers – we calls the police the crushers 'cos they wants to stamp their big boots on us and crush us like cockroaches. But they is mostly too addlepated and tossicated to catch us.

cullies – this is what I calls my friends.

D

dabs at – all us gutterlings has something we is good at. The tumblers is dabs at cartenwheels, I is dabs at telling stories of an evening, and Stick is dabs at coming up with plans and wheezes. Although truth be told, I reckon my wheezes is mostly better than his.

daffy – another of them words for a fool.

dandy – if something is dandy, it's just the best.

dib-dabs – this is what we calls them ten clever little things on the ends of our hands, what are dabs at dipping pockets and prigging stuff. The other word for them is fidgets.

dibs – don't be daffy and think this is something to do with your dib-dabs, 'cos it actually means money. Us gutterlings never have much money, but we has got lots of words for it, like 'mint-sauce', and the 'needful' or the 'necessary'.

dicey – never believe a cove what's dicey, 'cos he can't be trusted.

dimber-damber – this means going about the streets quick and smart, without causing any bobbery and bother.

dolly-tub – when Black Bill's missus gives me a wash twice a year, she fills the dolly-tub up with cold water and dunks me in it. A dolly-tub is what most people wash their clothes in, but I ain't never known her bother herself too much about that.

doolally – you might be wondering how many words we need for daft. I reckon you can't have too many, another one will always come in handy.

dumbflustered – this is what I calls it when someone gets so confused that it makes them daft and doolally.

F
fandangled – this is a word for something fancy and new. I loves going up the fair, 'cos there's always some clever cove up there what's invented something fandangled to cod the crowds out of their mint-sauce.

fettling up some kind of wheeze – this is what Stick and I is dabs at, coming up with a plan to make us some mint-sauce or some prog. But some wheezes don't work out too well.

flam-doodle – a bucketful of nonsense.

flummery – trust me, buttering a cove up with a bit of flummery and flattery has got me out of a few tight spots. But if that don't work, it's best just to run away. Fast.

frazzled off your fidgets – I've frazzled my fidgets a few times when I've prigged a meat pie too hot from the oven. Worth it though, when you gets a lick of that gravy.

G

gee-gaws – them pretty jewels make my mouth water, 'cos they is worth a barrow-load of meat pies.

getting in a pucker and a fluster – all hot and bothered and mad as a wet hen.

gigglemug – this is what someone who is addlepated looks like – they never stops smiling.

gizzard – this is one of the first words Black Bill taught me when I was first 'pprenticed. I was five and he said he'd cut me from my guts to my gizzard if I didn't get up the chimbley. I didn't wait to find out that he was talking about my throat.

grampus – this is a whale – I ain't never seen one, but Tree and Cess said they saw one what had got beached down the Thames and it were bigger than King Billy's palace. But I reckon they was lying like flatfish.

grinders – your grinders are what you use to chew up your food. If you're lucky enough to get some.

gutterling – this is what we call ourselves, 'cos we lives in the gutters. It's politer than what other people calls us.

gutter-perch – this is what we call sparrows, or spadgers, 'cos they perch in the gutters, next to us. Reckon they is even hungrier than us, most times, so if we has a crumb to spare, we gives it to a spadger.

H

half-inching – you needs lots of words for stealing stuff, in our line of business.

half-seas over – we also need lots of words for drunks, 'cos we're always falling over them in the gutter.

havey-cavey or havey-shavey – there's always plenty of shifty, shady coves lurking about, what you wouldn't trust further than the end of your nose.

His Nibs – this is what we calls the toffs and the swells.

humdinger – really good, the best.

humdudgeon – you knows to keep clear of a cove when they is in a humdudgeon, 'cos they is in a stinker of a bad temper.

I
in a flim-flam – this is what happens when you get in a pucker and a fluster.

J
jobberknoll – the streets are full of jobberknolls what are addlepated and loose in the attic.

junket – this is a wobbly pudding, like jelly but made with milk. I sees them in shop windows oftentimes and they makes my mouth water.

K
kecks – this is what we calls trousers, I reckon it's 'cos it's easier to give a cove a good kick than if you was wearing some shummocky skirt.

knocking seven bells out of each other – thumping the living daylights out of a person.

L
lardy-dardy – this is a word for the toffs and the swells, or for anyone what's putting on airs.

larrup – the first day I was 'pprenticed to Black Bill, he promised he'd give me a good larruping every day. It turned out it meant a good thump, and he's always kept to his promise.

lobscouse – this is sailor's stew. They says as it has meat in it, but I ain't seen much evidence of that.

lob your groats – there ain't no polite way to say it: when you lose your lunch.

loose in the basket – this is another word for being addlepated and a jobberknoll, 'cos your basket is the same as your bonce.

M
mash it – oftentimes you need a quick way to tell someone to shut their clack-box and be quiet.

mingy – miserable, mean.

mint-sauce – we got plenty of words for money. In fact, we got more words for money than we ever have pennies in our pockets.

mirksy – a useful word for a dodgy, villainous-looking cove.

mithering – nagging.

mizzle – when your cullies tells you to mizzle, you know you'd best scarper and run away fast.

moke – a downtrodden old donkey.

mux – making a right mess of summat.

N
nibblish hungry – when I is nibblish hungry I really needs to get my grinders into a juicy meat pie or one of them bags of mystery, and I don't stop to ask what's in it.

nick-ninny – you can never have enough words for a fool.

nubble-headed – same as a nick-ninny, stupid!

O
off their chumps – loose in the basket, gone mad.

Old Scratch – the preachers is always going on about the devil – but I reckon there's worse on the streets of London to worrit about.

P
palaver – an awful lot of bother and to-do.

pandalorum – a right mess and a bit of a pickle.

pedlar – some cove who goes about the place selling ribbons and stuff. I ain't never felt the need for ribbons.

plum duff – a steamed pudding, what's supposed to be full to bursting with plums but oftentimes you has to beg for the plummiest bits, or you end up with nobbut the steam.

pokey – sounds the same as chokey, and that's what it is – another word for prison.

to prig – when you liberate stuff from its rightful owner without the dabs to pay for it. Best get your cullies to keep an eye out for the crushers while you're at it.

prog – food or vittles – what we never have enough of.

pushing up the daisies – another word for being dead and buried, 'cos you end up under the ground and feeding the worms.

Q
quod – if you don't watch out for the crushers when you're prigging stuff and dipping pockets, they'll clap you in quod and there ain't no way out but transportation to 'Stralia or the gallows.

R

ripsmasher – really great, summat what knocks everything else into a cocked hat.

S

sapskull – an addlepated idiot what's got nowt between his ears.
shotten herring – a herring what's well past its prime. Don't eat one, or you'll be lobbing your groats.

shummocky – horrible, rubbishy.

skinflint – a cove what's so mean that he'd skin a louse for the sake of its skin.

slow-top – a sapskull or an addlepate what's about as cunning as a dead pig.

slumdinger – a slumdinger is as great as a ripsmasher – the best ever.

snabble – if you get snabbled it means you've been kidnapped – or worse.

snaffle – this is the same as prigging. Don't let the crushers catch you doing it.

stuck his spoon in the wall – if you stick your spoon in the wall it means you won't be needing a spoon no more, 'cos you've snuffed it. You is brown bread.

sweepling – I started as a sweepling in the chimbleys when I was nobbut five years old. You has to be small to be a sweep's 'pprentice – and it's in nobody's interest to let you grow bigger. That's why they don't feed you.

swell – this is what we calls the toffs, what prance about London in their carriages with their lardy-dardy airs. It pays to butter them up, 'cos now and then they'll toss you a ha'penny.

T

termagant – a right bossy old woman.

toe-rag – someone who's so disgusting they're worth no more than a stinking old cloth you wrap round your foot.

toff – same as a swell. Now and then a toff will toss us a ha'penny. But mostly we has to encourage them to be charitable, by picking their pockets and helping ourselves to their purses.

togs – clothes. I ain't never had much in the way of togs.

tootuk – this is ship-talk for the deck.

tosser – a coin, mostly the way we get our dib-dabs on these is if they is tossed to us by a toff, or if we picks their pockets.

tossicated – there's an awful lot of coves what are very fond of gin, and what ends up tossicated and half-seas over.

totty-headed – this is another of them words for daft and stupid.

trot-box – this is what the toffs drive about in, splashing mud over the crossing-sweepers and oftentimes crushing a gutterling or two under the wheels.

tumblers – the tumblers turn cartenwheels and chuck handsprings for the toffs to make them laugh, in the hope of a penny or two being tossed their way.

twig – catch on quick.

V

varmint – a bad cove. Not to be trusted.

vittles – this is another word for prog.

W

weevily – weevils are evil little insects what burrow into food and leave little holes. They loves biscuits best, but then, who don't love biscuits best?

wet around the winkers – winkers is your eyes, so I reckon you can work this one out for yourself. I don't know, 'cos I never cry.

the woefuls – if you have the woefuls you is miserable and full of the mulligrubs, and you needs to pull yourself together and stop snivelling.

ACKNOWLEDGEMENTS

I owe a huge thank you to my agent, Lisa Babalis, at Curtis Brown, for believing and for keeping that faith, and to my editor Lena McCauley at Hachette, for all her energy and enthusiasm and wisdom. Oh, and for the orange origami tiger which she gave me when we first met, which has sat on my desk ever since. Also to Emily Thomas, James McParland, Alison Padley and the rest of the team at Orion/Hachette for all their hard work and dedication in making *Tiger Heart* the best it could possibly be.

The Arvon Foundation promises that something magical happens on its writing courses; for me it was a coming home to story-telling, after long years away. Those blissful weeks in Devon and Yorkshire felt like a permission to do what I have wanted to do, ever since I first found out at the age of five that you could open a book and instantly be anywhere.

A special thanks to author Catherine Johnson for her generous and wise advice, and the Curtis Brown Creative team for their support.

My children, Scott and Holly – and now Sarah and Alexander – have always encouraged me, and kept me going (often with cake) on days of doubt. Holly is always my first and most trusted reader – she has to put up with me sending her stuff just because I have made myself laugh. Sorry about that. I also owe her an apology for stealing her stories when she was little. It's a good job she has so many stories of her own, now.

I said thank you to my mum and dad at the start of this book, but I could never really say thank you often enough. So thank you again, and always.

Almost forgot. The cats. Bruin, Snufkin, Oliver, Sassy, Molly, Milly and last but by no means least, Bonnie and Betsy. All of them, like Dr Johnson's Hodge, very fine cats. Very fine cats indeed. And to each and every one of them I owe a little bit of the Tiger.